Whisked Away

MAGNOLIA COVE MAGIC
BOOK ONE

NOEL BAILEY

Edited by Milly Bellegris and Halima Tobria

Proofread by Megan Cox

Cover design by Bring Design

www.authornoelbailey.com

For Jacki

Some people find their best friends. Some people get a sister. I got both.

Without your unwavering support, encouragement, and belief in me, Magnolia Cove wouldn't exist. Thank you for always cheering me on, for every brainstorming session, and for being the kind of sister who makes life a little more magical.

This one's for you.

Author's Note

Hey there, lovely reader,

Welcome to *Whisked Away*! This book is full of all the things I love most—slow-burning chemistry, small-town magic, and a romance that feels as cozy as a well-worn bakery apron. But it also dives a little deeper, touching on themes of trust, ambition, and the way our pasts shape the futures we dare to dream of.

You can expect plenty of humor and heart (because what's life without a little laughter?), a touch of mild language, and a few swoon-worthy moments where sparks fly. There's also an intimate scene on the page—poetic rather than explicit—but if that's not your cup of tea, I wanted to give you a heads-up.

At the heart of it, this is a story about love—the kind that sneaks up on you, challenges you, and ultimately makes you braver than you ever thought possible. I hope you find joy, warmth, and maybe even a little bit of magic within these pages.

Welcome to Magnolia Cove. I think you're going to love it here.

With love and a freshly baked cinnamon roll,

-Noel

Music Playlist

A playlist that feels like golden sunlight spilling through a bakery window, tastes like cinnamon sugar melting on your tongue, and hums with the spark of an impossible love. These songs are the perfect soundtrack to Alex and Ethan's story—where rivalry meets romance, big city collides with small town, and a little bit of magic changes everything.

Click here to listen now!

Alex

"Spellbinding Scones."

My editor slaps a gaudily bright magazine onto the desk between us, then follows up her statement by reading the subtitle. "Magic-infused baked goods served up in an equally charming Southern oasis."

It takes an entire twenty-three seconds—which I spend silently counting as I breathe deeply to lower my heart rate—before I pick up the publication as though lifting a damp newspaper from the gutter.

A sticky bun glimmers on the cheap, glossy cover. Rainbow frosting drips from the confection, like one of my childhood school folders exploded all over the monstrosity. Scones covered with gold and pink sprinkles rest on either side —presumably to prop up the sugar abomination.

My teeth hurt just looking at it.

"This is disgusting." I shift, my dress gliding against the black leather chair.

A fluorescent light flickers, highlighting Vivian's frown as she gestures for me to hand the magazine back to her, which I do.

"Perhaps so, but this is also selling."

A pigeon sits on the eave outside the window behind her, preening. It finishes the job, then flies away—out into the maze of skyscrapers, honking cars, and chewing gum-splattered sidewalks. At least the bird is free, even as it breathes in the smell of exhaust and burnt hot dogs from street vendors.

Unlike me—sitting in a high-rise office, food magazine covers with my name printed large and hung in expensive frames on the wall, while my editor flicks through a publication that isn't even in the same stratosphere as ours.

Suddenly, I'm annoyed. I put on a proper dress for this meeting. Packed my briefcase that can fit my laptop, cell phone, power bank, SLR camera and massive macro lens, cosmetic bag, non-toxic peppermint hand sanitizer, water bottle, and two tasteless protein bars in case the train breaks down like last time.

I dragged this hella heavy bag fifteen blocks for Vivian Ellison to hand me a copy of *Foodie Frenzy*.

"The masses like garbage. We've never bothered with flash-in-the-pan articles before. We write for a higher-brow audience."

My hands itch to reach for the folder perched on the desk. It contains the article I spent months researching. Spent another three nights combing through it for grammar errors like I was arranging flowers on a cake for a royal wedding. I even added a flourish, penning the title in calligraphy: *The Revival of Ancient Culinary Techniques in Modern Gastronomy.*

That was a piece of media worth consuming. It high-lighted real bakeries producing food with actual heart and history—like Eman's tiny three-table café, where he crafts fragrant Aish Baladi flatbread served with honey hummus he hand-makes in a wooden mortar each morning. A shop that will have a line stretching around the block once this article goes to print.

"Well, our readership is down." Vivian is serious now, her arms crossing and putting creases into her pressed blazer. "Really down, Alexandra. The board says we have to make a lane change."

I stand, wobbling slightly on my low heels because I also stupidly bothered putting on real shoes for this meeting. "That sounds like a marketing issue."

"Marketing can't sell what people aren't interested in buying. It's time for us to update. *Gastronomy Eats* has been touting the same articles for fifty years."

"They're classic and will stand the test of time."

The only reason I don't yank my bag up like a shield is that my shoulder still throbs from the walk. Instead, I run my thumb over the ring Mother gave me, tracing the worn metal like it's some kind of lifeline. Usually, it steadies me, reminds me that I'm capable. Not this time. This time, my hand shakes.

I clawed my way up to a salaried position at *Gastronomy Eats*. Busted my butt flying all over the world, turning in twice the articles than any other writer, making sure they were flawless, sacrificing five years of sleep. I've seen what happens when ambition takes a backseat to love, and I swore I'd never make that mistake.

And now, Vivian, standing there in her nine-hundred-dollar heels, is telling me my work—my career—is outdated? That people would rather read about rainbow-colored sugar bombs and so-called magic than real food journalism?

My head spins and I have the urge to press my fingers against the desk, leaving my prints stained on its shining surface.

Vivian tilts her head, the light catching the streaks of silver in her chignon. She's everything I'm supposed to become—

successful, independent, in control of a prestigious publication. Because success means security. It means never wondering if the bills will get paid, never gambling stability on something as fickle as love. Never making my parents' mistakes.

"So... what? We just—" I wave my hands at the trashy magazine again. "Start writing clickbait now? And there's no way in hell that photo isn't edited within an inch of its life."

Vivian doesn't blink. Instead, she flips open the magazine, manicured fingers gliding over the glossy pages until she lands on one, her nail tracing a line of text.

The only thing sweeter at The Whimsical Whisk than the pastries is the owner, baker, and certified magician, Ethan Hart. If he's not transforming butter and flour into the perfect pie crust or practicing a bit of scrumptious magic, he's volunteering with his local Boys and Girls Club.

She spins the magazine toward me, and my stomach drops before my brain fully catches up.

Oh, you have got to be kidding me.

"That's a gimmick." I jab a finger at the picture of *Ethan Hart*. As if that's a real name.

"Okay, this is clearly a gimmick. There's no way in hell that man knows a damn thing about baking."

The man staring back has an infuriating mix of charm and confidence—golden-brown hair curling against his forehead, eyes too bright, too blue, too full of warmth and mischief. And those arms—muscular, tanned, peeking out from a perfectly fitted T-shirt and a pale-blue Hedley & Bennett apron.

I have the same apron in charcoal. And it has never looked that crisp.

"That man"—I jab at his photo again, as if he's single-handedly responsible for all my life's problems—"is a paid actor. I mean, he says he bakes with magic, for god's sake. Plus, he looks like a firefighter from a calendar I once had."

Vivian closes the magazine with a knowing smirk. "Five years I've known you, and I never would have pegged you as the type to own a sexy firefighter calendar."

Heat crawls up my neck. I duck my head to hide the blush as I mutter, "We all have our indulgences."

Especially those of us with zero love life and no intention of getting one. I've spent my entire adult life building a career —because stability, money, and control are what matter. Love is reckless, unreliable. I saw what it did to my parents, the way it left my sister and me in a precarious financial situation.

Love led my mother to cut her hours to part-time, my father to take less prestigious work that didn't pull him away from our family, and both of them to choose an expensive suburb so my sister and I could have the best.

Now I'm stuck desperately trying—and failing—to find the balance between making enough to survive, providing for my sister, and doing something that doesn't suck my soul away.

All thanks to love.

I had one serious relationship, and it ended exactly as I suspected it would. Anthony wanted me to focus less on my career, more on our relationship. But I'd already seen how that played out for my parents. No amount of emotions could compel me to sacrifice security for a pair of sad puppy eyes, no matter how compelling they were. No matter how much it hurt to watch them fill with tears when I ended things.

Romance is like the rainbow-puke cinnamon roll—super sweet for a moment but guaranteed to leave you with a nasty stomach ache soon after.

So, I'll keep my firefighter calendar and the side of judgment if I must.

"He's a fake. The actual owner of this bogus bakery probably hired him because he has a pretty face."

"Likely," Vivian says. "But that pretty face is selling magazines—and lots of them."

"*Gastronomy Eats* is going to cover a fake restaurant with the corniest gimmick ever?"

Vivian scoffs. "No one said we'd be covering them. We want you to travel, spend a week or two in Magnolia Cove, and expose them. Then write a criticism that will take them off the map."

I stand to my full height and pull in a deep breath. My father had been an art critic, and his one bit of advice to me was never to build a career on tearing others down.

It'll leave you miserable, Alex.

Despite everything—the bills, my younger sister relying on me, the overwhelming responsibility—I've never compromised on that. I've poured my heart into finding new, promising eateries, then giving them press coverage that changed their lives.

"I don't know if I can do that."

Vivian frowns. "We have to turn the ship around and write pieces that will attract a new audience. If we don't, I'm afraid we'll need to make cuts soon."

My breath catches. Her implication is clear.

I can't lose this job. It's steady. I'm doing something I'm passionate about—for real money. Few people are lucky enough to get that.

Most importantly, Missy's senior year of college has brought enough expenses that I could have already started my own freaking restaurant. A little place of my own—cozy, intimate, where every dish tells a story. A dream I've shoved to the back burner so many times, it might as well be cold by now. But I vowed not to let her graduate saddled with debt and regret. Only one of us should have to live with that.

I have to keep this job.

"If I do it?" I ask.

"Then I imagine we'd strongly consider you for the next senior editor position."

My palms grow so sweaty I long to wipe them on my dress. Everyone in the office knows I want that position. It comes with a significant raise—enough to take some of the pressure off.

Still, I don't want my name on an article that trashes someone's restaurant, no matter how ridiculous it is. Being associated with something so banal is the last thing I need.

"I'll think about it."

"Do. I'll need an answer by tomorrow."

"Tomorrow."

I grab my bag with slick hands, sling it over my aching shoulder, and walk out into the buzzing office space.

* * *

"But you hate editing."

The train rattles, and I save my phone from sliding off the seat where it's propped to charge before responding to Tish.

"Everyone hates editing."

"Hmm." Dishes clatter in the background, and I picture her gathering up mugs in her tea shop, a rag in her other hand swiping away the crumbs from her zodiac cookies.

"I'm pretty sure some editors enjoy their job."

"Or maybe they all lie."

A man walks past, an umbrella looped over his arm, banging against every seat as he moves. I shift closer to the window to avoid impact, watching greens blur together outside.

I know Tish is right. Plenty of people love editing. But it's not for me. It's tedious, heavy with responsibility, and leaves little room for creativity. Managing a team when I can barely manage myself most days feels like a prison sentence. I want to run screaming in the other direction, but I need the money.

My breath fogs the window.

"Or maybe,"—she stretches the word out—"you should see this for what it is. A wake-up call. Smell the organic chai, girl. The tone of your voice says everything."

"My voice says I'm tired."

She's probably standing beneath the twinkle lights and fake moss strung above the counter, giving me side-eye.

"No, it says it's time to actually follow your heart for once. How long have you wanted to go freelance?"

My eyes shudder closed. Forever. That's how long. But hustling as an influencer for money only works if you don't have a mountain of bills and someone else relying on you. I shut the door on the idea of my dessert blog, *Tell Me Something Sweet*, long ago—though I still stupidly pay for the URL year after year.

Tish's teasing voice pulls me from my mental spiral. "Drop by the shop. I'll give you a reading. The leaves know everything."

I smirk, shaking my head, saying nothing, but her rich laughter tells me she already knows my answer.

Even if I don't believe in lucky stars, I thank them all for leading me to write a feature on Tish's cafe, *Celestial Sips,* four years ago. We disagree on basically everything, but somehow, it works.

The train stops, and I rise, grab my bag, and exit with the crowd.

"That reminds me—have you heard of Ethan Hart?"

Her squeal has me jerking my head back, as if I can escape my headphones.

Shuffling past the dozen others exiting onto the platform, I follow the crowd toward the stairs. My steps are careful on the too-steep concrete, my impractical shoes proving an even worse choice with every step. By the time I reach the sidewalk and head toward my apartment building, I regret them for the thirtieth time today.

"You mean the hot-as-hell baker with the magical bakery? He's all over the ClipClop app."

I kick a piece of gravel, watching it hit the crack in the station's brick wall. The train pulls away, and the murmurs of the dispersing crowd fade.

"It's a gimmick," I say. "It has to be."

"Or maybe the Universe is asking you to give faith a chance."

Reaching my building, I jog up the steps, the concrete clacking beneath my low heels. I pull out my keycard and swipe it at the scratched-up reader, waiting for the familiar buzz before pushing through the heavy glass door. The small foyer smells faintly of coffee and rain-dampened concrete, the fluorescent light flickering in protest as I pass through.

The building is close to the station, which means it's loud all hours of the night, but it's also affordable and convenient. At some point, the blare of a train whistle announcing its arrival just became part of the background noise.

"Well, the Universe is definitely giving me a shove." I grunt as I drop my bag to the ground, fish out my keys, and let myself into the apartment. "*Gastronomy* wants me to spend a few weeks in Magnolia Cove."

"Oh my god, you lucky bitch."

Laughter spills out of me as I drag my bags inside, barely making it past the doorway before shoving them into the corner. I can worry about unpacking it later. That's officially future-me's problem.

"Alex!"

Missy closes the fridge and whirls around.

I point at my headphones and speak to Tish. "My sister's here. I'll have to let you go."

"Tell her I said hi. Oh, and give the Universe a chance for once. This might be your lucky break."

Sure, it might. Writing a trash piece about a tourism gimmick is exactly how I'll achieve all my hopes and dreams.

"I'll do that," I answer, to her laughter, before digging out my phone and hitting the end call button.

Missy leans against the counter, a can of carbonated water in hand. Her thick, blonde hair is braided over her shoulder, and she has all the curves the Universe never blessed me with. Despite that, I still have a hard time seeing her as older than twelve. An eight-year age difference can do that to siblings, I guess.

"You're home early."

She grins, her fingers denting the can. Her nails are pink, nearly matching her dress. Keeping them short is a necessity for a cellist. Despite her talent, it still shocked me when she got accepted into Juilliard. Or maybe that was just the sticker shock.

I vowed she wouldn't walk out of school with six figures of debt, but it feels like it's slowly sinking me.

One more year and she'll graduate.

Something about her energy is vibrating, and I can't tell if it's excitement or nerves. I walk past her, open the fridge to grab a carbonated water for myself, then turn to face her.

"Spill. Whatever it is, just tell me."

Inhaling sharply, as if it's her final breath, she sets the can down on the cluttered counter. Books are stacked in haphazard piles, sheet music is tucked between photo props, and a candy thermometer rests in a mason jar next to metal skewers. You'd think we cook more than we do, given the amount of kitchen paraphernalia we own. It's my guilty pleasure.

"First of all, I want to say I plan to pay for it." Missy looks me in the eye as she says this, and I force myself to breathe, to count, to keep my expression from wavering. She practically shimmies. "I've been invited to spend my last semester at Schola Cantorum!"

My mind shuffles through the names of music institutes. That one doesn't ring a bell, but it definitely doesn't sound like it's on this continent. "Is that in Europe?"

Missy's smile breaks across her face—the before-Mom-got-sick smile. "Yes, in Paris! Isn't that thrilling?"

More breathing. More counting. "Absolutely. And how much is the tuition?"

She drops her arms against the counter, takes a sip of her strawberry water, and moves the can so the condensation ring sparkles in the light. "I'm going to take out a loan."

"Absolutely not."

"Alex." Her voice turns whiny, and suddenly, she's seventeen again. Our mom is gone, and in one painful swoop of fate, I've become her legal guardian. Dad had passed barely a year before, and with no other family to lean on, it was just the two of us. "I really want to do this."

"Okay, then you'll do it."

This is her dream. She's worked her butt off for three years, kept her grades up, and excelled at music. She's going to be somebody one day, and it's stupid that money should hold her back. I'm sure this study-abroad program will come with another five-figure expense, but I'll find a way to manage it.

Never mind that I'm barely keeping up with our regular expenses, that we live in a crappy apartment an hour outside the city because it's all we can afford, and that medical bills sucked up what little our parents left behind.

None of that matters. Missy shouldn't have to carry that weight. If there's one good thing fate freely gave me, it's my sister. I'll do anything to protect her.

Besides, I'll make it work.

I shrug, like I actually believe the BS I'm feeding myself. "I spoke with my editor today, and it looks like I'm up for a promotion. It'll probably be just enough of a raise to make this work."

"Wait, seriously?" She runs around the counter and wraps me in a massive hug, her vanilla-scented shampoo filling my breath. Pulling her tight, I tangle my fingers into her hair.

My anxieties wash away. This is what really matters.

"Oh my god, congratulations! You've been overdue for it —no one works as hard as you, Alex." Missy pulls back. "Tonight we celebrate! I won't take no for an answer."

She twirls away like a ballerina, laughter trailing behind her as she disappears into her bedroom. I can only hope that by *celebrate,* she means splitting a bottle of wine over the restaurant leftovers I shoved in the fridge.

My heart flutters—an irritating little skip—before my stomach does a full, unwelcome dip. I shove the feeling aside and picture Missy in Paris, learning from the best musicians in the world, drinking in the city like it was made just for her.

Why should she give that up? Why should she drown in debt just so I can avoid torching some con artist's bakery?

People say there's no such thing as bad press. If anything, a scathing article in *Gastronomy Eats* might actually boost the shady little operation in Magnolia Cove.

I roll my eyes at the thought. I'm pretty sure all the names are completely made up.

With a sigh, I grab my bag, digging out the copy of *Foodie Frenzy* I picked up at the train station. The pages are already bent from my grip, but I flip straight to the one that started this mess.

Ethan Hart stares up at me, that damn twinkle in his eyes. He's clearly a talented actor, and I hate to risk ruining his current schtick—but we all have bills to pay.

Running my thumb over the cheap, glossy paper, I notice a detail I'd overlooked.

Ethan Hart has dimples.

My heart and stomach do that weird thing again, but I practice my favorite hobby—lying to myself—and chalk it up to lingering anxiety.

Narrowing my eyes, I jab a finger at the overly perfect man's photo. And then, in my best food-critic voice, I say to him, "Well, Mr. Hart, I'll be seeing you soon."

Ethan

There's no quiet like the silence of a bakery at three in the morning, and there's no noise like the same space at seven-thirty when everyone stops in before rushing off to work.

I love them both.

The Whimsical Whisk buzzes with people this morning—the usuals, like Mrs. Delehay, who always brings her Pomeranian in her handbag, which I pretend not to notice. Rachel and Grant, who still act like they're newly in love on their morning muffin date. Or Charlie Luck, who's eight and has a bigger sweet tooth than allowance. My assistant, Zoe, slips him freebies by the end of the week, and I pretend not to notice that too.

It's the tourists that captivate me, though. People are surprising when it comes to baked goods.

A man in a button-down linen shirt—one step away from dressed for a business meeting—will walk in, give a *what the hell, it's vacation* shrug, and order a cinnamon roll he'll eat with his fingers.

Or a family of five will file in, select a slice of cake, and quietly eat it in micro-bites over the course of half an hour in the booth by the window.

Tourists always bring bits and bobs with them too—a magazine discarded on a table, discussion of a sugar brand I've never tried, candy that isn't sold on the island.

As much as I love The Whimsical Whisk—and I love the hell out of it—I adore the plank ceilings, the hunter-green cabinets I painted myself, and the yeasty smell that has customers closing their eyes and taking a deep breath when they walk through the door, jangling the bell. But despite that, the island it's on isn't just a home for me. It's a prison.

A reality I'm reminded of by Dean Markham hanging around today, sipping on a free coffee and making small talk with a few of the locals. He's tall and lean but muscular, with serious dark eyes that flit around the place—their color matching his black tee and jeans. I don't know how many damn times I've told him he makes tourists uneasy. He's ignored it just as often.

Sliding cookies out of the oven, my hands slip, and the tray crashes to the floor. I curse under my breath. Dean has a tendency to throw off my focus.

"I got it." Zoe drops beside me, gathering up the fallen cookies with fingers used to heat, tossing them into the trash bin. She's pulled her purple-streaked hair into twin braids today. "Why don't you take over the register?"

"Thanks, Zo." I grip her tattooed arm and trade places with her. I've been lucky to have her working with me for the last three years. There are few others in Magnolia Cove as interested in early hours and the peculiarities of baking as I am.

Slowly, the morning shuffle passes through. Zoe and I pull bread dough out of the fridge and prepare it for baking— loaves that locals will pick up this afternoon to eat with soup or scrambled eggs, and tourists will purchase for a picnic on the tiny stretch of sandy beach just outside of town.

Dean finishes his coffee, tosses the cup in the trash, and chews on a toothpick until everyone's gone. With a sigh, I exchange a look with Zoe before removing my apron and walking around the counter.

"Something I can help you with?"

Dean rolls the toothpick back and forth like he's attempting to grate on every single one of my nerves. He's a smashing success, as always. "Dropping by for my monthly check-in."

His voice is gritty. It's a wonder people trust him any more than me. Though, he's a warlock—one of the most important members of magical society, since they create the wards that keep humans from noticing magic in pocket towns like Magnolia Cove. And they have the magic to stop monsters. Like me.

"Here I am."

"It's the Lunar Occultation tonight. Shop's open anyway, I notice."

I struggle against grinding my teeth. "And everything is going normally, isn't it?"

"Fine, fine." He takes the toothpick out of his mouth, snaps it, and tosses it aside. Then he drags a rolled-up magazine from his back pocket. "Have you seen this?"

It hits the table with a slap, the garish colors glaring up at me. My neck heats as a copy of this month's *Foodie Frenzy* unfurls, the rainbow-colored pastry clashing against the warm tones of my bakery.

Yes, I'd seen that embarrassing article. I knew the woman who wrote the piece would focus most on the magic-infused marketing. I didn't realize she'd Photoshop the images until they looked like a circus spectacle.

We needed a gimmick to draw tourists to the island. The

mile stretch of sandy beach wouldn't do it when there were far better and more accessible shores on the mainland. Visitors funded the local economy, and smart marketing brought more of them to our town.

So why not lead with the truth? The baked goods *were* magic-infused—not to change their flavor or texture, but to leave the person eating them feeling satisfied, peaceful.

Most of the island's foods were similarly touched with magic.

Dean had disapproved of the ploy when I started the bakery. But who would believe the magic was real? No one, especially thanks to the wards that kept any humans from seeing Magnolia Cove's reality—kept them from remembering anything other than the good feelings when they left our shore.

I hadn't realized I'd turned my baking—my one pride—into a joke.

I shove the magazine aside. "It's an article. The council approved this."

"I don't like the word *magic* showing up next to *Magnolia Cove* so much." Before I can reply, he continues, "The entire warlock and witches' council doesn't like it."

I deeply regret already taking off my apron—I could have used the excuse of removing it to hide my reaction. "They approved my petition. Besides, the article is already out there."

He steps closer to me, his black boots out of place in the bakery or on the island itself. But he's Dean Markham—he gets away with whatever he wants.

"Should I remind you," he whispers, "about the cost and time of having to do the repair work when our magic ends up out there?"

I could take this man in a fight. For all his muscles and sharp looks, he's better with words and magic. I'm no warlock—my body doesn't possess magic I can infuse into spells, making me a demigod like Dean. But it possesses an inhuman amount of brute strength and fighting intuition. My fingers curl, but I force them to straighten.

I can't risk everything I've built here over Dean.

And if I screw up, they won't just kick me off the island—they'll throw me into a real prison pocket community. A place with no way out, where rule-breaking magic users are locked away for life. Magnolia Cove might have its limits, but at least here, I can still breathe.

Dean's right, anyway. I burned my shot in the human world. Fell in love. Had my heart broken. And in the aftermath, let too many people see too much of the magical world.

Witches and warlocks had to clean up behind me.

Now, all I have to do is survive twelve more months of good behavior, and I'll finally be able to shake free of Dean as my parole officer. Maybe in another five years, they'll even let me take a few short trips off the island.

A man can dream.

Until then, I have *The Whimsical Whisk*. And I won't risk it for anything.

"I get it." My voice is steady, but it takes effort. "This article is probably a good thing, anyway. It makes magic seem comical. Besides, Foodie Frenzy? No one takes it seriously."

Dean grunts but doesn't argue. Instead, he rolls the magazine up again, then pulls a folded envelope free that's been folded into thirds and shoves it at me.

"What's this, then?"

I snatch the envelope and unfold it, my breath rushing from me as my eyes land on the byline.

Gastronomy Eats.

It's addressed to me.

"That's some sort of big production, isn't it?"

The envelope crinkles in my grip. Dean has no idea. *Gastronomy Eats* isn't just big—it's *the* biggest food magazine in the country, maybe even the world. It's built careers, put restaurants on the map, and is taken seriously by every major name in the industry.

I should know. I subscribe to it.

"It has a niche audience," I say, keeping my voice even.

"Make sure that whatever comes of this"—he taps a finger hard enough on the envelope that a corner slips from my fingers—"we maintain our secrets. Be more mindful of what you say to the press this time."

His dark eyes flick up to mine, a silent warning in them. I stare back, refusing to yield. He may be my keeper, but that doesn't make me his lapdog.

With a scoff, he moves past me. "I'll see you at the same time tomorrow."

Before I can respond, he's through the door, the bell jingling. Tourists veer away from him—whether from his demeanor or some subconscious awareness of the magic emanating from him, I don't know.

Oven timers ding. Zoe lifts massive trays filled with half a dozen doughy loaves and slides them in. I should tuck the envelope away and help, but I can't stop staring at it.

Someone at *Gastronomy Eats* wrote to me. It's probably too much to hope that they want to feature the Whisk in a story. Damn, I'd take a side panel or even just a mention. If two lines about my bakery make it into the magazine, I'm cutting them out and framing them.

With trembling hands, I open the envelope and pull out the letter. I read it once, then again.

"Something wrong?" Zoe slides the last tray of bread into the oven and resets the timer, her brow knitting as she studies me. "You look like you just found out buttercream was outlawed."

I force a smile and lift the paper in my hands. "*Gastronomy Eats* sent me a letter. They want to send someone here to interview us. They—" I swallow hard, barely believing the words as they leave my lips. "They want to write a *feature* on us."

Zoe's reaction mirrors the one I must have worn just moments ago. The color drains from her skin, making her tattoos stand out in stark contrast. Her lips part, but no sound follows. For a long beat, the bakery holds its breath with us— the steady hum of the ovens, the warm, yeasty scent curling through the air, the soft swish of the air conditioning the only things filling the silence.

Then, she lets out a whoop so loud it startles a pair of tourists outside. She throws her hands up and leaps clean over the counter, crashing into me with a hug. The impact knocks me back a step, but I return it just as fiercely, grinning like an idiot.

We've done it. Even within the tight confines of our world —the secrecy, the rules that keep us hidden, the way Magnolia Cove can feel more like a gilded cage than a sanctuary—we've managed to catch the attention of a serious magazine.

My mind races with possibilities. I have recipes I've poured my soul into but never shared. Maybe they'll publish some. Maybe this will bring enough visitors to the island to not only help us but our neighbors, our friends.

Zoe pulls back just long enough to snatch the envelope from my hands. She skims the letter, her eyes widening before she lets out a sharp whistle. Then, with zero shame, she launches into an impromptu happy dance—hips wiggling, envelope flapping in the air. A few passersby stop to watch, some amused, others baffled. Not that it bothers her. Nothing ever does—a quality her wife finds both charming and mildly exasperating.

"Did you see who they're sending?" she asks.

I take the letter back and smile, my heart doing an

unsteady little flip. I'd already read the name. I'd already panicked—and celebrated—over it.

"Alexandra Sinclair."

Gastronomy Eats isn't sending an intern. They're sending one of their top writers. Her stories grace the covers more often than not. She's not just a writer—she's a storyteller. She takes the most intricate processes or simplest food stories and weaves them into something unforgettable.

I tried macarons again after swearing them off forever because of an article she wrote about a French family who'd been making them for five generations. I still hated the cookies —too pretty for how disappointing they actually taste—but we can't agree on everything.

"I'm going to ask her exactly one million questions," Zoe says.

"You absolutely will not."

She doesn't answer, just grins in that *oh-but-I-absolutely-will* way.

"This is about the Whisk, Zo. We need to position ourselves just right. This could be our one big opportunity." Our chance to make an actual impact. The gimmick had drawn in more tourists, but maybe we could do more than that. Maybe I could make a real mark on the culinary world— even from my gilded cage.

"Mmhm." She barely pays me attention as she unties her apron.

"You've got the bakery for the next hour, right?"

"Sure. You leaving?"

"I've got to go tell Mia, duh." She drags her apron over her head and tosses it at me. "Oh, and your dad and Tom and Rhianna. If I tell Rhianna, the entire town will know by closing time."

"Zoe, wait, maybe we should—"

But she's already out the door, waving and grinning before skipping down the sidewalk.

Dean, still chatting with someone outside the window, turns and shoots me a glare. Gaining extra attention from him when he's already in a pissy mood and it's one of the most dangerous days of the year for me isn't a great idea.

Oh well. It's worth it.

I lost my freedom acting stupidly with a human woman.

Now, another human woman might give me the chance to gain something even more important.

Freedom.

I run my fingers over the name. *Alexandra Sinclair.*

"See you soon, Ms. Sinclair."

Alex

Magnolia Cove is a postcard town.

No, scratch that. It's worse. It's the kind of place that exists solely in Hallmark movies, where everyone knows everyone else's business and the biggest drama is whether the annual pie contest will have a surprise winner this year.

As I step off the ferry, my low heels clack against the weathered wooden dock, and I'm hit with a wall of saccharine sweetness. The air is thick with the scent of honeysuckle and sea salt, mingling with what I swear is the aroma of fresh-baked bread.

It's nauseating.

I adjust the strap of my laptop bag, grateful I had the foresight to ship most of my luggage ahead. The last thing I need is to be dragging a suitcase through this Norman Rockwell nightmare.

Fourteen days of my life I'll never get back, all to write about some gimmicky tourist trap masquerading as a quaint bakery. I think longingly of the article I should be writing—some hole-in-the-wall shop I could discover instead, the kind that serves fourth-generation recipes made with heart and talent a person can't learn in a single lifetime.

"Welcome to Magnolia Cove!" a cheery voice cries. I turn toward the woman who could be the poster child for small-town tourism. She's got a clipboard in one hand and a smile that belongs in a toothpaste commercial. "Are you here for a day trip or staying a while?"

I force a smile that feels more like a grimace. "Two weeks, actually. I'm here on business."

Her eyes light up like I've just told her I'm giving away free puppies. "Oh, how wonderful! You must be the writer everyone's been talking about. From that big food magazine, right?"

Everyone's been talking about me? Great. Just great. So much for keeping a low profile and getting an honest look at this place. As soon as I step into the shop, Ethan Hart is going to know who I am. That's if he even actually works there. They'll probably have to notify the actor and have him arrive. Maybe I can get ahead of the gossip if I see the bakery first thing.

"That's me." Beyond the woman, old oaks line the street, blocking most of the town's view. But bits of white buildings peek through, and a clock tower soars above their branches. "Now, if you could point me towards—"

"The Whimsical Whisk? Of course! It's just down Main Street, you can't miss it. It's the cute little shop with the teal awning and the most delicious smell coming from it. Ethan's cinnamon rolls are to die for!"

"Thanks," I offer, readjusting the bag on my shoulder. My heels click as I transition from the boardwalk to the cobblestone street, and I already regret my footwear choice. I thought them inconspicuous, modest even, but compared to everyone else walking around in loafers and cork sandals, I'm definitely overdressed.

Everything is so quaint it hurts. Flower boxes overflow

with bright blooms, and every shop has a clever name that probably took the owner weeks to come up with. I pass A Novel Idea bookstore and The Mane Attraction salon.

Tish would love it here. She'd drag me into every single shop and insist the entire place was adorable. She wouldn't be wrong. But something about it feels too perfect. There's not a scrap of peeling paint or a crack in a single brick. No dirt sullies the colorful doorways, and the gutters are completely leaf-free.

It's like I've stepped onto a corny holiday movie set. I'm waiting for the cameras to appear as I approach the cheery teal awning that flutters in the ocean breeze.

The smell hits me before I even reach the door. It's intoxicating—warm, sweet, with hints of cinnamon and vanilla. For a moment, I forget why I'm here. It reminds me of my first time in Cancale. Everyone always wants to write about the Paris baking scene. Few acknowledge the little coastal towns filled with dozens of family-owned bakeries, each with their own unique specialties—like the crispy butter cookies, Galettes Bretonnes, that made me rethink the entire concept of what a cookie was. Or a prune tart I had at another shop, called a Far Breton, that made me reconsider the idea of using prunes altogether.

My stomach growls, reminding me that airplane pretzels do not a meal make.

I shake my head, clearing it. I'm not here to be charmed by some mass-produced, pre-frozen dough. The Whimsical Whisk is no boulangerie. I'm here to do a job—to show the world that there's more to food than social media-worthy swirls of food coloring.

As I reach for the door handle, it swings open from the inside. A wall of muscle and flour collides with me, and I stumble backward, my laptop bag slipping off my shoulder.

Strong hands grip my arms, steadying me. Firm fingers

grasp my bag's strap, keeping it from colliding with the ground. I look up, ready to unleash a biting comment, but the words die in my throat.

Blue eyes. The bluest I've ever seen, framed by laugh lines and a dusting of faint freckles across a strong nose. The man attached to those eyes is unfairly handsome, with tousled curls that look like they belong in a shampoo commercial and biceps straining against his flour-dusted T-shirt.

It's Ethan Hart. The cover model turned fake baker. He's even more attractive in person, which only serves to irritate me more. Of course they'd hire someone who looks like him to front their operation. It's all about appearance over substance. I'm mostly annoyed that he actually works in the shop and I didn't catch them without their act in place.

"I'm so sorry!" he says, still holding my arms. His voice is deep, with a hint of a Southern drawl I refuse to find charming. "Are you all right?"

I open my mouth to respond when I notice the tray on the ground between us. Pastries have scattered across the cobblestones, some still intact, others smashed beyond recognition.

"Oh no," Ethan mutters, releasing me to crouch down. "I'm such a klutz. These were for Mrs. Delehay's bridge club."

"Well," I say, finding my voice at last, "it would seem Mrs. Delehay doesn't prefer the rainbow extravaganza that's been gracing magazines lately."

His face snaps up, those crystal-blue eyes widening slightly. A flush spreads over his cheeks so deeply that his freckles stand out like a constellation. Before he can respond, a laugh erupts from inside the bakery.

"Smooth move, Teddy Bear!" A woman with vibrant tattoos running down her arms leans against the doorframe, grinning. "Is this how you greet all the pretty tourists? By assaulting them with pastries?"

Ethan's cheeks darken even more, and he stands, brushing

his hands off on his apron. "Zoe, this isn't—I mean, I didn't—"

"Relax, Boss." Zoe continues to grin. She turns to me, extending a hand. "I'm Zoe, by the way. Welcome to The Whimsical Whisk, where the service is a little clumsy, but the pastries are to die for. Usually not literally, though."

I shake her hand, surprised by her firm grip. "Alex," I say, hoping they haven't recognized me and that I might have a chance to explore the bakery without them realizing who I am. "Charmed, I'm sure."

Ethan's eyes widen. "Wait, Alex... as in Alexandra Sinclair? From *Gastronomy Eats*?"

I clench my teeth to hold in a groan. Tish would say I'm losing my touch. *You need more rest. A good cup of tea, a reading of the leaves, and listening to the Universe for once in your life,* her voice echoes in my mind.

I force a smile to mask my grimace, smoothing down my blouse—now thoroughly rumpled from the impact. "That's me. The culinary world's most notorious pastry assassin."

With a dramatic sigh, I gesture toward the fallen treats, their once-delicate forms now nothing more than crumbled remains strewn across the sidewalk. Overhead, a few birds perch in the tree, their beady eyes locked onto their next meal, waiting for the perfect moment to swoop in. "Exhibit A."

Zoe's grin is instant, her hazel eyes dancing with amusement. "The murderer has revealed herself. It's the world-renowned food critic with the laptop bag on the sidewalk. I'll let Col. Mustard know he's off the hook."

Despite myself, I can't help but laugh. Zoe is several inches taller than me, wearing a cutoff tank beneath her apron. Her purple-highlighted black waves are twisted into a messy bun atop her head, and splatters cover her smock—though none of them are rainbow-colored. In fact, despite the Whisk's magical reputation, there's not a hint of neon or glitter in sight so far.

Ethan runs a hand through his flour-dusted hair. "I... we weren't expecting you so soon. I mean, we knew you were coming, but..."

"I prefer to feel out a place on my own at first. It's nice for my initial impression to be the same as any other customer's."

Ethan looks as if I've just informed him that his car needs a loan-worthy repair one day out of warranty. His mouth falls open, and his brow knits into furrows, pushing away his perfect, magazine-model expression. It almost makes me want to reach out and pat his arm.

Maybe he does actually care about this hokey bakery.

Surely he can't believe *Gastronomy Eats* is going to write a genuine article about this circus act and his *to-die-for* cinnamon rolls, which are probably covered in enough neon frosting to summon a troll.

Ethan nods and gathers up the broken pastries. "Of course. Well, um, would you like to come in? I can show you around, maybe offer you some samples?"

I straighten my laptop bag and sling it back over my shoulder. Then, I readjust the strap, making sure nothing got damaged. My initial plan was to observe from afar, but now that they know my identity, perhaps a direct approach is better.

Plus, I can't deny that the aroma wafting from the bakery is tempting.

A part of me wants to reach out, to reassure him. Despite his towering frame, he seems to match the 'teddy-bear' nickname Zoe dubbed him with as he bends down to collect the pastries. The birds above eye him disapprovingly.

But I'm not here to soothe Ethan, the cover-model-turned-bakery-worker.

I'm here as a journalist. A sister who's holding on by a thread, hoping she doesn't lose her job. A provider who's clawing for a promotion, a raise, a future.

And what *Gastronomy Eats* wants is clear: expose this place for the overpriced, overhyped tourist trap that it is.

"I suppose so," I reply. "Though free samples can't influence my write-up, of course."

Ethan's smile falters for the briefest of moments, before snapping back into place. It's too perfect. Too warm. Too sweet. Just like this town.

He holds the door open for me. "Wouldn't dream of it."

As I step inside, the warmth and the aroma hit me all at once—like a cozy, intoxicating hug.

I brace myself against the charm offensive.

I have a job to do. Bills to pay. A story to write that'll move me up to the next level in my career.

And if this place—and these people—end up hurt by the truth? Well, that's the cost of progress.

Despite the fact that Zoe's energy reminds me of the first time I met Tish... and Ethan seems surprisingly... authentic?

They work at a tourist trap. Even if it stings their pride, this article will be my ticket to better opportunities. To authentic kitchens that deserve the spotlight—places where my words could change lives, preserve food culture, and push people to explore something new.

That's my focus.

And if I have to wade through sugar-coated hell to get there? Well, so be it.

Ethan

I've been staring at the same batch of scones for ten minutes, willing them to bake faster through sheer force of will. It's not working.

"You know,"—Zoe leans against the kitchen island—"I don't think your magic works that way, Boss."

I shoot her a look. "I'm not using magic. I'm just... thinking."

"Uh-huh. And does your thinking usually involve that much forehead sweat?"

I swipe at my brow, grimacing when my hand comes away damp. "It's hot in here."

"Sure it is." Zoe grins, her maroon lipstick shimmering. "It has nothing to do with the fact that you literally knocked over a top writer at *Gastronomy Eats* half an hour ago?"

My stomach does a backflip. Alex. Alexandra Sinclair. The woman I embarrassed myself in front of, ruining what was probably an expensive outfit and definitely her first impression of me and The Whimsical Whisk.

"I can't believe that happened," I groan, turning back to the scones and checking their color. Almost ready.

Zoe shrugs. "Could've been worse. At least she didn't sue you for assault with a deadly pastry."

I glare at her. "Not helping, Zo."

"All right, fine. Take a breath, Sugar. It's not as bad as it seems." She peers over my shoulder at the scones. "Those for her?"

I nod, then slide on oven mitts as the timer dings. "Along with the cinnamon rolls and the lavender shortbread."

"Trying to break her sweet tooth on day one? Cause her stomach distress and distract her with bigger problems so she forgets that shaky first impression? Bold strategy."

I ignore her, carefully removing the tray and setting it on the cooling rack. The aroma fills the kitchen with notes of vanilla and orange zest. They look perfect—golden brown with a slight sheen from the egg wash. But looks aren't enough, not for Alexandra Sinclair.

I close my eyes, take a deep breath, and let a tendril of magic flow from my fingertips into the scones. It's subtle, barely noticeable unless you know what to look for. A faint shimmer, like heat rising off pavement in summer. I infuse them with warmth, comfort, and a sense of home.

Everyone on the island can tap into General Magic. Only the powerful can do the things most people think of as *magical*—create wards, alter memories, shape-shift. But the bakery doesn't need those kinds of powers. A kiss of comfort is enough.

When I open my eyes, Zoe is watching me with an uncharacteristically serious expression. "You sure about this, Ethan? Dean's already on edge about the publicity."

I remove the oven mitts and hang them on their hook. "What choice do we have? If I don't use magic and help take the edge off, she'll write us off as just another tourist attraction. If I do…"

"We risk exposure," Zoe finishes. "Damned if we do, damned if we don't."

"Exactly." I grab a plate and arrange the pastries. "But maybe, if we can impress her enough, she'll focus on the quality of the food rather than the gimmick."

Zoe snorts. "Yeah, because journalists are known for their ability to ignore a juicy angle."

She has a point, but I'm not ready to admit defeat just yet. We had a poor start, but while we infused baked goods at The Whimsical Whisk with a touch of magical comfort, it didn't alter their taste or texture. I'd spent years perfecting my cinnamon roll dough proofing. I special-ordered the muscovado brown sugar from the Philippines. And I added a tablespoon of orange rind—not enough to notice, but just enough to contrast against the sweetness. I was obsessive with my tests and never released an item on the menu until I was fully confident in it. The Whisk's offerings could stand on their own—if she'd let her critical eye drop for a moment and actually try them.

"Just... keep a watch on things out there while I finish this up, okay?"

"Sir, yes sir." Zoe gives a mock salute before sauntering out to the front.

I take my time arranging and rearranging the pastries, making sure each one is positioned just so. It's probably overkill, but I can't shake the feeling that everything is riding on this first impression. Well, *second* impression, if you count our disastrous meeting earlier.

Finally, I emerge from the kitchen, plate in hand. Alex has set up camp at a corner table, laptop open, a look of intense concentration on her face. The morning sunlight streaming through the window catches in her hair, turning it to spun gold.

I shake my head, banishing the poetic thought. This

woman is here to judge us, maybe even expose us—or, though I hardly dare to hope, significantly boost our profile. I'd imagined her coming to write one of her cover pieces, but her tone has shifted my suspicions. Why would someone like Alexandra Sinclair write an article about the Whisk? She wouldn't. Now my brain can't stop imagining the food criticism section in the back of *Gastronomy Eats*.

With all that in mind, I can't afford to get distracted by the way she bites her lip as she types.

"Special delivery," I say, approaching her table.

She looks up, her lip unfurling from her teeth's clasp, her hazel eyes turning honey. "That's quite the sample."

"Consider it a peace offering," I say, setting the plate down. "For, you know, assaulting you with pastries earlier."

A hint of a smile tugs at the corner of her mouth. I wasn't sure what I'd expected from Alexandra Sinclair, but this woman somehow isn't it. For one thing, I'd expected her to be older. To write for *Gastronomy Eats* at her age is impressive. She must have worked her ass off to reach this position. Yet her smile says there's more to her than just a stodgy food critic.

I'm trying very hard not to notice the cupid's bow of her lips or the way a strand of hair slips forward and brushes her skin. Yet, I find my gaze lingering a moment too long on the curve of her neck as she looks up from her laptop.

"Well, I won't say no." That smile graces her lips again. It makes my heart race, and I'm pretty sure it's from the dread that she might hate the Whisk. Hate it, and write about it in an article that slaps my name and face in front of every person I'd ever hoped to gain respect from. She could ruin every one of my dreams—the dream of becoming a true expert in the field, the kind of baker whose name is studied in culinary schools, whose cookbooks sit dog-eared on the counters of professionals. Someone who isn't just a gimmick, but a master of the craft.

I hold my breath as she takes a bite, watching for any sign of the magic taking effect. For a moment, nothing happens. Then I see it—a slight softening around her eyes, a barely perceptible relaxation of her shoulders.

"This is..." she starts, then stops, cocking her head at the pastry.

"Not what you expected?" I offer.

She shakes her head, taking another bite. "It's good," she admits, sounding almost reluctant. "Really good, actually."

Pride surges in my chest but is quickly tempered by the knowledge that this is just the beginning. One good scone will not be enough to win over Alexandra Sinclair. Not if she came here looking for the worst. I'm already mentally preparing to go home tonight and comb through every copy of *Gastronomy Eats* I own to analyze her critiques.

She nudges the cinnamon roll but doesn't rip into it. "I'm surprised this doesn't look like something out of a kid's birthday party—all neon frosting and sprinkles."

My hands grow clammy, and my magic shifts within me. Too many potent emotions can cause me problems, especially around the Lunar Occultation—when celestial shifts make magic unpredictable, pulling at it like tides. I clear my throat. "I didn't take you as a *Foodie Frenzy* reader."

She folds her fingers together and rests her chin on them. "I'm not."

"Me either."

Her frown is so scathing that heat spills up my neck. My magic trembles within me and I take a deep breath. "Well, unless they provide free advertising, I guess. Tahitian vanilla doesn't buy itself," I say lamely. All I want to do is escape to the kitchen and pretend like I won't replay the conversation in my head until I throw up. I gesture at her laptop. "I'm keeping you from working. Let me know if you need anything else."

As I turn to go, she calls out, "Actually..."

I look back, hoping my expression doesn't betray my desperate desire to escape. "Yes?"

"I was wondering if I could ask you a few questions. About the bakery, your background, that sort of thing."

"Of course." I glance at the counter, wishing a line would magically appear. Instead, Zoe is cleaning the glass case and shoots me a not-even-trying-to-be-discreet thumbs-up. I pull out a chair and sit across from Alex. "Glad to share anything you want to know."

It's a lie, of course. There's so much I can't tell her, so many secrets I have to keep. About Magnolia Cove, the Whisk, and myself.

"So, Mr. Hart," Alex says, her fingers poised over the keyboard. "Tell me about the 'magic' behind The Whimsical Whisk."

I freeze for a split second, my mind racing. This is going to be harder than I thought.

Before I can formulate a response, Zoe appears at the table, coffee pot in hand. "Refill?" she asks brightly, even though Alex's cup is still mostly full.

Alex looks up, startled. "Oh, that's okay, I'm—"

"Great!" Zoe says, topping off her cup anyway. "I gotta say, you're younger than I expected. And prettier."

A faint blush creeps up Alex's neck. "I... thank you?"

"Don't mention it," Zoe says with a wink. "So, what do you think of our little town so far? Bet it's a far cry from the big city, huh?"

Alex's professional demeanor slips for a moment, revealing a flash of something—something brittle. "It's... quaint," she says finally.

Zoe laughs. "That's a polite way of saying 'painfully adorable,' right? Don't worry, it grows on you. Like a fungus."

To my surprise, Alex actually cracks another smile at that.

Maybe I should stop attempting to interact with her and let Zoe take over.

"I'm only here for a couple of weeks," she answers. "Not much time for fungal growth."

"A couple of weeks?" Zoe echoes, shooting me a meaningful look. "You'll miss the best part of Magnolia Cove's summers if you leave then."

I clear my throat. "Well, I'm sure Ms. Sinclair has other assignments to get to—"

"Alex," she corrects. And there's that look again—I'd almost call it vulnerable if I didn't know better. It makes me want to ask her questions, discover if she has secrets of her own.

"Right, Alex," I say, the name feeling strangely intimate. "We're just grateful that you came across the Whisk and decided to visit."

Zoe gives a wink and sashays back towards the cash register as a cluster of people walk in, bedecked in beach cover-ups and streaks of sunscreen. She's busy convincing them of the merits of cake on hot days in a way that only Zoe could pull off.

Alex flicks her eyes back to me. "Now, about the magic that the internet can't stop talking about..."

"Right," I say, frantically trying to come up with a plausible explanation that isn't an outright lie. "Well, you know what they say—a good baker never reveals all his secrets."

It's a weak deflection. Alex frowns slightly, and her fingers curl tighter against her keyboard. But before she can press further, the front door dings again. It's usually a cheerful sound, part of the Whisk's charm, but Dean Markham strides in and his dark eyes scan the room until they land on our table.

My stomach drops.

"I'm sorry," I say, standing up. "I need to take care of something. Zoe can answer any other questions you have."

Alex looks like she might stand as well. She readjusts and

takes a delicate pinch of the cinnamon roll. And because of our glaring visitor, I don't even get the chance to see her reaction as she takes a bite.

As I hurry toward Dean, Zoe strides over to Alex and launches into one of her signature stories—this time, about the time she accidentally set off the bakery's fire alarm. Not with fire, but with a disastrously smoky batch of burnt caramel. "Ethan told me to watch it closely, so I did," she says, deadpan. "For a full five minutes after it had already turned black."

I half-listen, a smirk tugging at my lips. Zoe has this uncanny ability to turn her worst moments into her best stories. It should keep Alex entertained for a few minutes.

"What is she doing here?" Dean hisses as soon as I'm within earshot.

"Her job," I answer, keeping my voice low. "She's a food writer, Dean. This is what she does."

"We agreed to a puff piece for a tourist magazine," he snaps. "Not some in-depth exposé by a top publication."

I run a hand through my hair. "What do you want me to do? Turn her away? That'll only make her more suspicious."

Dean's jaw clenches, his frustration mounting. "I want her trip cut short. Let her sample the food, write her article, then tell her to leave."

"I can't just—"

"You can, and you will," he cuts me off. "Unless you want to risk more magical exposure. Risk everyone else in this community by following your heart again."

His words hit harder than I'd like to admit. The truth is, he's right. I wanted more than the magical community could ever offer, and that desire had caused enough legal chaos to fill an entire file cabinet at the Witches and Warlocks Council.

"I'll figure something out," I mutter.

With that, Dean turns sharply and storms out of the

bakery, leaving me standing there—pulled in three directions: my duty to the town, my professional ambitions, and the lingering shame of my past mistakes.

With a heavy heart, I head back to the table. Alex looks up as I approach, her smile lighting up her face in a way that makes my heart skip a beat. I push the feeling aside, reminding myself of the risks, but there's no denying the flicker of hope that ignites within me. This could be my shot —my chance to show the world what the Whisk is really about.

Others won't find out about the magic. I'm more in control now. Dean just loves worrying about something. And I just happen to make a good punching bag.

"Everything okay?" Alex asks, concern creeping into her voice.

I force a relaxed smile. "Just an island tourism issue. Nothing to worry about." The half-truth feels off, but it's the best I can offer.

"Great," she says, turning back to her laptop. "I was going to say, 'Where were we?' but we never made it past the first question. The magic that makes up the Whisk."

Her eyes glisten with the warmth of sunlight—but it's more than just that. It's curiosity. The kind that could get us both into trouble. It's probably what makes her such a damn good journalist—her ability to unearth the tiny details that make readers feel like they're right there with her.

I can't lie to her anymore. I won't. But I can't tell her everything either. So, I'll do the only thing I can: give her just enough to satisfy her curiosity, and pray it's enough to keep her from digging deeper.

I shrug, aiming for nonchalance. "You know, my Nan always said it's about the love you bake into something." The words come out sounding more cliché than I intended, and Alex's fingers stop clacking against the keys.

"Love, huh?" she says, her tone dry. "That's your secret ingredient?"

The trite answer has disappointed her. But maybe that's for the best. The less intrigued she is, the safer we all are. Still, I can't help but feel a pang of regret as the sparkle in her eyes dims.

"Well, that and a few family recipes I'd be skinned alive for sharing, plus a dozen years of experimenting." I gesture to the plate of nibbled-on pastries. "Some things have to remain a mystery, you know?"

Alex leans back in her chair, studying me with those sharp eyes. "Mr. Hart, I think you'll find I'm very good at solving mysteries."

There's a challenge in her voice that makes my pulse quicken. Part of me wants to rise to it, to show her everything the Whisk—everything I—can do. But Dean's warning echoes in my mind, and I feel the familiar prickle under my skin that warns me to stay in control.

"I don't doubt that," I say, keeping my tone light. "But some secrets are worth keeping, don't you think? Leaves a little magic in the world."

Her lips thin, but she doesn't press further. Instead, she closes her laptop with a snap. "Well, I suppose I'll just have to do some more... thorough investigation during my stay."

The way she says it makes it hard for me to force a smile. I don't know how to convince this woman to leave early, to ask her not to go nosing around in things. "I spent a year in Paris and learned quite a few of my tricks there."

This gathers her attention again. A few local kids come in and walk over to the cookie case. They press their hands and noses against it, and Zoe sighs, but says nothing. That glass remaining smudge-free is a splinter under her nail, always bothering her, but she loves the kids too much to say anything about it.

"Who did you train with?" Alex asks.

I suddenly wish I had a cup of coffee and could wrap my hands around it, fidgeting with the handle. I've made a mistake. She won't find my experience there impressive. "No one you'd know. A few of my neighbors were natural-born bakers. Or maybe it was generations of family secrets. I charmed them into sharing a few with me."

She takes another bite of the cinnamon roll and chews it thoughtfully before answering. "My sister is about to study in France."

Probably with a real institution, not 'I baked galettes with a few French grandmothers, and that's the magic behind the bakery featured on Foodie Frenzy.' God, this has to be the least impressive assignment she's ever had. I regret—not for the first time—coming out of the kitchen for the day.

"Where at?"

"Schola Cantorum. She's a cellist. Talented too."

She brightens when discussing her sister, but my stomach twists. Of course, her sister is going to some prestigious-sounding institute. I didn't know where Alex studied, but she likely had an impressive background. Where I saw Magnolia Cove as laid-back and charming, she likely saw an unremarkable coastal tourist town. And the baker she was sent to write about? Someone who thought baking frequently made him an actual professional.

"That's amazing," I say, because it is. "I hope she enjoys her time there."

I had. Paris was magic—but dark magic. Purse cutters waiting in shadowy corners were as common as the scent of freshly baked baguettes wafting over the Seine. It had an edge to it that Magnolia Cove lacked. The kind of edge someone like Alexandra Sinclair probably appreciated.

The only thing we have to set us apart is magic.

But she can't find out about that.

As Alex gathers her things to leave, promising to return tomorrow for more 'research,' I catch Zoe's eye across the room. She gives me a thumbs up and a wink, clearly thinking I've charmed our visitor. If only she knew the turmoil churning inside me.

Alex walks out the door on heels, her styled hair bouncing against her shoulders, the bell chiming cheerfully behind her. I'm considering removing the thing. Alex writes beautiful, sharp pieces filled with unique angles and a story that sucks you in.

She won't find that in Magnolia Cove—not if I throw her off like I must. She'll end up seeing us—me—as unappetizing as the nearly full plate of sweets remaining at her table.

Alex

The next morning, I stroll down Main Street, notepad in hand and camera slung around my neck, but I can't shake the feeling that something's... different here. I've been in towns like Magnolia Cove before. Or at least, I thought I had.

Tish had texted me earlier. *How's paradise and the hot baker?*

A bit too picture-perfect, I'd texted back while I had limited service at my bed & breakfast.

She'd sent a rolling-eye emoji but followed with, *Try to have fun for once!*

I pass by a quaint flower shop, Petal Pushers, where a petite woman with a crown of ivory braids arranges a bouquet in the window. She looks up, catching my eye for a moment before quickly averting her gaze. Odd. I don't know how Tish expects me to enjoy my stay in this strange little town. She'd love it, though. It's a shame she couldn't join me.

My first real stop is *A Novel Idea*, the bookstore I noticed yesterday. As soon as I open the door, I'm enveloped in the comforting smell of old paper and leather. An orange tabby cat stretches, hops out of the window, then rubs against my leg. I bend down and run my fingers through its soft fur. "Well, hello, you."

Missy wanted a pet. I'd held firm on my decision against one. We couldn't afford another dependent, and it would end up alone too often.

"Welcome to *A Novel Idea*," a deep voice calls out. "Let me know if you need any help finding your next literary adventure."

The man who turns toward me could have stepped right out of a romance novel cover. Tall, dark, and handsome doesn't even begin to cover it. He's perched on a rolling ladder, shelving books with the reverence usually reserved for holy relics. First Ethan, now this guy—was there some kind of 'ridiculously good-looking business owner' requirement in Magnolia Cove?

"Thanks," I say, approaching the counter. "Actually, I'm here more for information than books. I'm Alex Sinclair, from *Gastronomy Eats* magazine. I'm doing a piece on Magnolia Cove and was hoping to chat with some locals."

The man's eyebrows shoot up, and he descends the ladder with surprising grace for someone his size. "Well, well," he says, extending a hand. "Marcus Blackwood, at your service. I'd be happy to chat, though I'm not sure how much help I'll be with a food article."

I shake his hand, noting the calluses that speak of a life not just lived behind a counter. "You'd be surprised. Sometimes the best stories come from unexpected places."

Marcus grins. "In that case, what would you like to know?"

Before I can start my questions, the bell chimes again. A woman enters, her arms laden with a tray of muffins.

"Special delivery for my favorite boss," she announces softly.

Marcus' expression turns soft. "Mia! Perfect timing. Come meet our town's latest visitor."

Mia sets the box on the counter, her caramel braid sliding over her cardigan. I don't know how she's wearing a sweater in the summer, but she doesn't seem to have even broken a sweat.

"Oh, you must be Alex," she says. "Zoe mentioned you when I dropped by the Whisk."

"Zoe is very friendly."

Mia snorts as she hands a muffin to Marcus, then arranges the others onto a glass dish by the register. "My wife has never met a stranger, that's for sure."

Marcus hasn't peeled the paper back from his muffin yet. I want to watch him take a bite—to see if Ethan Hart's confections impress the locals as much as they impressed me. After the first taste of the tart, I'd struggled to maintain my professional expression.

Layers.

Endless layers of flavor had burst across my tongue.

He had the texture perfected as well. Many tarts would end up soggy with such a generous filling. Not Ethan's though. The crust was crisp against the sweet center. Some flavor notes I couldn't quite figure out set off the sweetness.

It had taken all my self-control to not inhale the entire plate. As a food writer, I'd had to learn early on to appreciate bites and nibbles. The palette was at its sharpest when hungry. I didn't like to fill up on food, but Ethan Hart's offerings were more than just food.

They tasted like comfort.

Like trekking with Missy as kids across the road to our neighbors where she taught us how to make pierogies, then plied us with sweets. Ethan's offerings demanded you sit and savor them, as one soaked up the Whisk's hand-painted cabinetry and golden glow. It was the kind of place a kid could sit and do their homework, or someone could take a date for breakfast, or where a person could cry with a friend after a breakup.

It felt less like a commercial restaurant and more like a home.

And the baked goods. They cried for someone to consume them slowly while sipping a warm mug of tea. Consider a second serving. Spend an entire afternoon lingering over them.

"Is there anything specific you're looking for?" Marcus asks.

I readjust my camera strap. They're both watching me, and I realize I've probably stared into space as I mused. "I'd love to read something about the town's history. Do you have any books on Magnolia Cove?"

Marcus and Mia exchange a quick glance before he gestures towards the back. "We have a few general history books. But Magnolia Cove's always been a hidden gem. Not much has been written about it, I'm afraid. We rarely get famous writers interested in our town."

He offers a smile that's so disarming, it feels fake.

There's a story here, and I can smell it as easily as the vanilla and blueberry wafting between us. I used to believe in charming towns and good-hearted people, but experience has taught me that every perfect picture has cracks—you just have to look close enough.

Marcus shoves his hands into his jean pockets. "If you have questions, I can do my best to answer them."

"That would be great!"

He offers a muffin, which I accept. My mouth has slowly filled with saliva as I've stood smelling them for the last few minutes. I follow him and Mia to a few leather chairs in the back corner and take a seat. The orange tabby jumps into Marcus' lap, and he pets her, but he seems distracted, his gaze distant.

"Where do you want to begin?" The way he asks is careful,

almost rehearsed. There's something hiding beneath Magnolia Cove's crust—something much more interesting than the story I thought I'd come to write.

"Tell me about Magnolia Cove's founding. It must have an interesting history."

He leans against the chair, his shoulders too broad for the wing-back. "Well, it was founded in... what was it, Mia? 1842?"

"1852." She crosses her leg, then seems to think better of it and rearranges so her houndstooth flats press into the carpet. "By the, um, Magnolia family, of course."

My pen hovers over the notepad, but I lift my face. "The Magnolia family? I've never heard of that used as a surname before."

She and Marcus exchange another look, and she chuckles. "Must be unique to the area."

"Are there descendants still in the area?"

"No," Marcus takes over. "I'm afraid not. They, uh, moved away pretty quickly. But their legacy lives on in the town's name, of course."

There's a wooden clock on the wall behind him, intricately crafted. The carved acorns click softly as they sway back and forth. "Right." I tap my pen against the still-bank notepad. "What brought the Magnolias here initially? Fishing? Logging?"

"Oh, a bit of everything," Mia chimes in. Her blush-pink fingernails grip her chair's arm. "You know how it is with these coastal towns. People come for the... opportunities."

Okay, then. I pause, trying to think of a direction to take the conversation. Usually, when people talk about their local area, they only need a few nudges before dishing up every flake of gossip and bit of little-known lore. I take a bite of the muffin and have to fight a shudder of pleasure.

The crumb is tender but structured enough to hold up to

the rich, buttery tones. It contrasts against the fruit's sweet and tart notes. And there's something else I can't quite place. Lavender, maybe?

"What about more recent history?" I try, setting the muffin down. I'll take it back to my bed & breakfast with me. "Any big events in the last few decades? Changes to the town?"

Marcus chuckles, but it sounds as hollow as an empty oven. "Oh, you know, small towns. Not much changes around here. We like it that way."

I scratch '1852' on the pad solely to have something to write. I'll purchase a book and see if it has more to say.

Mia sits up higher in her seat. "Except for the Whisk, of course. It's gaining a lot of attention currently. I guess you could say Magnolia Cove changed the day Ethan Hart moved here."

"He's not from Magnolia Cove, then?"

Marcus stands, causing the cat to jump from his lap. "Probably best to direct questions about Ethan to him directly. Everyone who isn't from the Cove moves here for the lifestyle."

"What lifestyle is that?" He seems even taller standing as I look up at him from my seat.

His expression softens again, the grin returning. "Laid-back. Magnolia Cove is a safe place. We have the beach, a great bookstore, if I say so myself"—I return his smile—"and now with Ethan's baked goods, some of the best cinnamon rolls on the East Coast."

Or the world, possibly. Not to be dramatic, but there's something about them that tastes like comfort—like returning home from school to fresh-baked cookies or curling up with Missy under a blanket as we devoured a boxed cake together.

Not that his food is subpar.

It's not.

It just has something else I can't name. Something that feels like home.

"Maybe I could buy some of those general history books you mentioned?" I ask.

Mia rises and gathers them. As she's ringing my purchases up, I lift a flyer. "Best cherry pie this side of the Mississippi?"

She looks at the sheet I hold, advertising *The Hungry Gull* —a local diner I hadn't seen yet.

"Oh, that's true." She places the books into a paper bag. "It even won the Blue Ridge Baking Championship last year."

"Really?" I ask. Marcus steps up behind Mia, and they exchange another look. I have a feeling she'd dish more if her intense, albeit handsome, boss wasn't around.

Mia shrugs. "We take food seriously in the South. Thanks for visiting A Novel Idea."

I accept the bag and keep the questions burning on my tongue from spilling out. I don't want to spook anyone away, but there's something off about Magnolia Cove. Off in a good way, if that even makes sense.

Soon, I'm back outside again, walking beneath massive oak trees that cast the sidewalk in shade. The ocean's breeze rushes through the space and rattles the leaves.

I frown at the slim volumes I bought. They were the only ones that mentioned Magnolia Cove's history. Most of the first book is about the general coastal region. There are a few paragraphs discussing the island's beach. The ferry that shuttles people to and from the mainland gets an entire page. But the history gets a single sentence.

Magnolia Cove was founded in 1852 by those who saw the potential in its wild beauty.

I tuck the books back into the bag and shift it under my arm. Here's a town I've never heard of that's producing award-winning pies. The Blue Ridge Baking Championship sounds niche, but it's a pretty big mark for a sleepy coastal island with no renown. How do they even get such fresh ingredients? Having supplies shipped has to add delays and complications. Most importantly: why isn't Magnolia Cove a foodie destination if the cuisine is this good?

The more I learn about this town, the less sense it makes. There's something here, something just beneath the surface that everyone seems to be in on but me.

I need to call Vivian later to tell her I'm going to need to extend my stay in Magnolia Cove. There's more to the story than I thought, and I can finish my other work remotely.

I'll have to work on the rest of my articles at the bed & breakfast. The town has extremely limited cell service and no wireless internet. It's as if it exists in a bubble, separate from the real world. If I do this right—not just a takedown, but a compelling, headline-worthy exposé—it could mean more than just a promotion. It could put me in the running for a James Beard Award or a National Food Writing Prize. The kind of recognition that could cement my name in the industry.

I catch sight of my reflection in a shop window. There's a gleam in my eye that I haven't seen in months—the thrill of a real story, a mystery to unravel.

Magnolia Cove may look like a postcard, but I'm starting to think it's hiding something much bigger. And I'm going to find out what it is and let the world know.

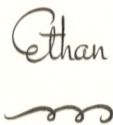

Ethan

The early morning quiet of the bakery is my favorite time of day. It's just me, the soft whir of the mixers, and the yeasty scent of dough rising in the proofing drawer. No customers, no Dean Markham, no Alex Sinclair making me question every decision I've ever made—or say more foolish things. No reminders of the life I lost, the one I should have had if I hadn't let my heart—and my magic—get the best of me. Magnolia Cove was a second chance, but it wasn't freedom. It was a leash, long enough to make me forget it was there until moments like these reminded me I wasn't really my own man. Not yet.

I'm elbow-deep in a batch of brioche when Zoe bursts through the back door, her black leather jacket flapping out like wings with the motion.

"Morning, Boss!" she chirps, far too cheerful for the ungodly hour. "Ready for another day of culinary deception?"

I grunt, focusing on the dough beneath my hands. Zoe, undeterred by my lack of enthusiasm, whips out her polishing cloth and heads to the display case.

"So," she says, her tone deceptively casual, "what's the plan for our favorite foodie today? More evasive non-answers? Or are we going for the full smoke and mirrors routine?"

I sigh and finally look up at her. "I don't know, Zo. I'm not... I'm not good at this. All I want is to make amazing baked goods and for more than just the five thousand people that live on this island to eat them. Maybe that's asking too much."

She slings her jacket off and hangs it on a peg before grabbing an apron. "Hey, no one's asking you to be James Bond here. Just be yourself. You know, minus the whole secret you can't tell anyone about that got you imprisoned here."

"Right," I mutter. "Just be myself. The non-magical, totally normal baker version of myself."

Zoe rolls her eyes. "You know, for a big teddy bear, you sure do overthink things. Look, why don't you just make her one of your special tarts? The raspberry ones always seem to put people in a good mood."

I freeze, my hands stilling in the dough. The Hopeful Raspberry Tart. It's one of my most potent creations, infused with just enough magic to lift spirits and soothe worries. Raspberries are back in season. Dad just brought me a dozen cartons from his hobby farm he had started since moving here. But using magic on Alex feels... wrong somehow. I spent the entire night regretting infusing the pastries I'd given her the day before. I say I want my baked goods to stand on their own, yet the minute they face real criticism, I don't trust them.

"I don't know, Zo. Isn't that kind of... manipulative?"

She snorts. "More manipulative than lying to her face? Come on, Ethan. It's not like you're brainwashing her. You're just... helping her see the best in things. Including you. And so what if it influences her review a bit? Would it be bad if a few more people visited and tried your cinnamon rolls? And before you interject, the answer to that would be no. The world is missing out. Plus, the boost in tourism to Magnolia Cove has been good for everyone. It's all under control."

I'm saved from responding by the front door swinging open. Alex walks in, her hair windswept and her cheeks flushed from the morning chill. My heart does a stupid little stutter that I would deny until my death.

"Morning," she says, her eyes landing on me. Maybe it's my imagination, but her gaze seems to linger longer than necessary. "Hope I haven't arrived too early."

"Good morning," I manage, suddenly very aware of the flour on my arms and the dough stuck to my hands. "You're welcome anytime we're here. We're always up before the moon sets."

"Me too, but for less romantic reasons. Journalism and regularly traveling in different time zones does bad things for sleep schedules."

Before I can respond, Zoe swoops in. "Well, you've come to the right place! Ethan here was just about to make his famous Hopeful Raspberry Tarts. You simply must try it."

I shoot Zoe a look, but she just winks at me before disappearing into the back.

Alex takes another step in. Her slacks have a crisp tailored line and not a single wrinkle; the sleeveless sweater she wears seems as exotic as Magnolia Cove must appear to her. No one wears designer clothes around here. "Hopeful, huh?" she says. "That's an interesting name for a tart."

I wipe my hands on my apron. "It's, uh, an old family recipe. Nan said it could lift even the gloomiest spirits."

"Is that so?" She lowers her laptop to the same table she sat at before. Soon, I'm going to think of it as Alex Sinclair's booth. "Well, I suppose I'll have to test that claim. For journalistic integrity, of course."

"Of course," I echo, my mouth suddenly dry. "Coming right up."

As I retreat to the kitchen, I can feel Alex's eyes on me. It's unnerving, like she seems to see right through me. Or maybe that's just the paranoia talking.

I lose myself in the familiar motions of baking, letting muscle memory take over as my mind races. The tart crust comes together under my hands, delicate and buttery. As I spoon in the raspberry filling, I hesitate for just a moment before letting a tendril of magic flow from my fingertips into the fruit. I infuse it with warmth, comfort, a sense of home and belonging. It's not mind control or anything nefarious—just a gentle reminder of good things.

As the tart bakes, filling the kitchen with the sweet scent of berries, I can't help but feel a twinge of guilt. Am I crossing a line here? But then I remember the suspicion in Alex's eyes, the way she seems determined to uncover secrets that could destroy everything I've built here. Everything this town has built.

I've already caused enough damage for our community. I don't want to cause them issues again. All I'd like is to have a chance to pursue my passion.

The timer dings, jolting me out of my thoughts. The tart that emerges is picture-perfect, the raspberries glistening like rubies. I plate it carefully, add a dollop of freshly whipped cream, and take a deep breath before heading back out front.

Alex chews her lip as she stares pensively at her laptop. It's distracting—too distracting. She looks up as I approach, and my breath catches. She's beautiful. Any fool would recognize that. And I certainly qualify for that category.

"Here you go." I set the plate in front of her. "One Hopeful Raspberry Tart. For journalistic integrity."

She grins, as if the joke wasn't the corniest thing I've ever uttered in my life. "It looks good. Let's see if it lives up to the hype."

My heart pounds as she takes a bite. The minutes seem to

tick by. Soon, the bakery will officially open, and the usual bustle will begin. Tarts and muffins, and dozens of cups of coffee, will be exiting with the customers. Alex chews the first bite thoughtfully. Her eyes close, and she freezes for a moment before swallowing.

"This is... wow," she finally says, taking another bite. "I don't know what I was expecting, but it wasn't this." She licks a stray crumb off her lip, and I force myself to look away.

"Good wow or bad wow?" I try to keep my voice casual.

"Definitely good. I feel... I don't know how to describe it. I haven't figured out how to describe your baked goods yet, Mr. Hart. It's a strange thing— a writer at a loss for words."

The guilt I felt earlier evaporates at the warmth in her tone. Maybe Zoe was right. Maybe this isn't manipulation, but just... helping her see the magic here. Helping her see that it's not a gimmick, even if she can't know the full truth.

"If you insist on me calling you Alex, then you must call me Ethan. We're not very formal around here."

Alex smiles and takes another small bite of the tart. She closes her eyes again as she chews, and the quietest moan escapes from her. I realize I'm staring at her lips when she opens her eyes once more. "I met Zoe's wife yesterday."

I need to return to the kitchen and not leave the entire breakfast rush to Zoe again, to stop indulging whatever draw Alex has for me, but her words pull me up short. "Mia is lovely."

"She seems so. She told me you're not from around here."

I fight a sigh. Mia is the sweetest person—vanilla whipped cream to Zoe's tart lime pie—but she's also quick to share anything. It's not because she's a gossip; the opposite, actually. She doesn't understand the purpose of lying. Zoe finds that as charming as a cookie's crumb, as she once said, but it presents a problem. Now I need to figure out exactly what Mia told Alex.

"That's true. I was born in a mountain town north of here. Always loved the ocean, though."

"Is that why a guy like you moved here, then?"

There's no half-truth to give her on that. I snag onto something else instead. "A guy like me? What does that mean?"

A pretty rose color spreads across her nose. "You know, all... capable-looking?"

"Capable-looking?" She's asked it like a question, but I don't know what she means. It doesn't sound like embarrassment or fraud, though, so I'll take it.

"I don't know... like a firefighter. Or a model. A firefighter model?" Alexandra Sinclair, renowned food writer, is sitting in my little bakery and blushing until she's pink in the cheeks. She covers her eyes with her hands. "Oh god, forget I said that. Something about this place makes me put my guard down."

I'm grinning stupidly, though. She'd described the island as charming, but I'm finding her even more so. "I'm willing to take it as a compliment. Just don't say it in front of Zo." I nod to where she's retreated, finishing the brioche. "She's dubbed me with enough nicknames. We don't need to add Chief to her list or have her explain the story to every single customer who comes in here."

Alex laughs, her eyes sparkling. Her computer has gone dark, but she doesn't seem to notice. "I'll keep it as our secret."

A pang grips my chest. I want to believe her. I wish I could trust her and know that secrets could stay between us. But I'd trusted a human woman before, and I'm still paying for it. Paying for it in years, in lost opportunities, in the weight of a promise I was foolish enough to believe. I slide a chair out and sit, feeling less bumbling. "The story of how I started baking isn't interesting enough for *Gastronomy Eats*. I've read your articles—you're always finding the most fascinating angles.

Like that story last winter about the Maple Syrup Farm in Vermont."

"Sugarbrook Farms." She clasps her hands together. "I loved writing that story."

She's watching me intensely, but now the words are flowing for me. Discussing the world of pastries and flaky crusts, the bakers out there pouring their heart and souls into their work is easy. "I loved how you discussed their use of traditional wood-fire evaporators and how it adds a smoky taste to their syrup. I ordered some after reading the article." She smiles at that, and it's like the expression is its own fire, warming me. "They have an interesting background. A family history of working with maple trees and unique techniques. Mine's boring."

"Try me." She takes another bite of the tart—a nibble, really. She eats things in the smallest tastes and chews each one thoroughly, as though she wants to give all her sensory attention to the flavor.

"I didn't grow up on a fourth-generation farm. The closest thing I have is I helped my grandmother in the kitchen. She had this oven that was ancient—I swear that thing was around before a mortar and pestle." Alex snorts, but she leans forward as well, drawing closer. "The smell of bread baking at her house was... well, like magic."

"That sounds lovely."

"It was," I say, surprised by the wistfulness in my voice. Surprised that I'm not ashamed to share this story with this polished, well-educated woman who has a sister about to spend a semester abroad. My story isn't anything special—I mean, except for the magical bits—but with this aspect, I can give her the entire truth. "She taught me that baking isn't about following recipes. It's about pouring your heart into what you create. About making something that might bring a little joy to others."

"Is that why she named it the 'Hopeful' Raspberry Tart?" She lifts a forkful of the pastry in question.

Not exactly, but it's also close to the truth. I shrug. "Food has the power to change how people feel. It can comfort, inspire, bring back memories—"

"Or create new ones." Alex sets the fork down, and it clinks in the silence between us. I'm not willing to break her gaze to see if Zoe is watching us, but I'd bet my secret banana bread recipe she is, and I'm going to hear about it later.

We've grown so close that with every breath, I catch the faint scent of her perfume mingling with the bakery's sweet aromas. At some point, without thinking, we both leaned in —just slightly—close enough that the space between us feels charged, like the moment before a first bite of something decadent.

I clear my throat. "So, how does a gal like you end up in our little corner of the world? And before you have to ask, I mean a successful, big-city food writer?"

She's quiet for a moment. Outside, the sky has woken, pink blooming its way over the trees. When she speaks again, her voice has lost its brightness. "I've grown tired of writing about pretentious restaurants where the portion sizes are too small, but no one will declare that the Emperor has no clothes. I've spent the last few years trying to find food and stories with heart. Something real."

"And then an embarrassingly corny article in *Foodie Frenzy* brought you here?"

My words come out a bit too forced. She's looking for something real, and she probably assumed we were the defini- tion of fake. Heat creeps up my neck, shame and regret washing over me as I think about that garish article. What must she think of us? Of me? I want to explain, to tell her that that's not who we are, that I got caught up in the potential benefits and didn't see the cost. But the words stick in my throat. I want her to see that The Whimsical Whisk is more than rainbow-colored gimmicks and flashy headlines. That there's real passion here. Real magic. And not just the kind that comes from our abilities. With *Foodie Frenzy*'s article as her first impression, I'm not sure I'll achieve that.

She taps the computer, and the light glows, making her skin pale and ethereal. "A fair point. I don't know, Ethan." The way my name sounds in her mouth is the same feeling I had the first time I mastered flaky layers in a croissant. "Sometimes people end up surprising you."

Hope bubbles in me like batter rising. That should capture my full attention. Instead, I'm fixed on the graceful way Alex lifts a fork, the gleam of her hair, the purse of her lips. She's certainly surprised me.

"Tell me more about your childhood with baking?"

I dash a quick glance to Zoe to make sure she doesn't need help. She makes a shooing motion, but her smirk says we are definitely going to discuss this later. Tucking that away for now, I return to Alex and let stories I haven't thought about in years unfurl from me. My initial disastrous attempt at croissants, the time I accidentally put my grandmother's favorite embroidered hand towel in the garbage disposal, the first contest I entered but didn't realize all the cookie bottoms were burnt until the judges spat them out.

Alex laughs, and the expression transforms her, brightening her face and easing her posture. I ask her questions, and she shares her own tales—of weird food trends she's had to review, of different people trying to make it in big cities with nothing but a few family recipes and a dream, and of misadventures with her sister.

Time slips away, and it's not until Zoe clears her throat loudly that I realize the morning crowd has arrived without me noticing.

"Duty calls," I say.

Alex types away at her computer but stops to meet my gaze. "You must go when called upon, Chief."

I laugh as I rise from the chair and say hello to a few locals. Mrs. Delehay tuts about the weather as she passes, clutching a piece of brioche against her heart.

"Ethan?" I turn back to Alex. She's golden and glowing, and she's eaten her entire tart. She lifts the empty plate. "Thanks for a bit of hope."

I only nod, but I want to tell her thank you for the same.

Maybe everything will turn out fine.

Alex

Magnolia Cove is driving me crazy.

Tish responds instantly. *Crazy good or crazy bad? Spill the tea! Is it the gorgeous baker you keep avoiding my questions about or the mysterious small-town thing? Or both! I need details!*

I stare at the message for what feels like an hour before typing out, *I'll have to call you soon! About to leave and have no service.*

Ughhhhh, is her dramatic but well-deserved response.

I don't know why I feel defensive of Magnolia Cove. My first night here, I called and complained about everything—grumbling into the B&B's old landline, since my cell service was useless—the overly quaint inn with its floral wallpaper and creaky floors, the way everyone seemed to know I was coming before I even arrived.

Now, just a few days later, I find myself wanting to protect this quirky little town and its inhabitants. Especially Ethan. The thought of trying to explain my change of heart about him through text feels impossible.

You'd think I was losing my mind, but I'll call you soon.

Honey, you've been losing your mind for years, is her response, followed by a kissing face emoji.

I tuck my cellphone into my bag, even knowing it won't work, as I head out into town. I've been here for four days, and I swear this place is gaslighting me. Everything is just a little too perfect, a little too quaint. And don't even get me started on the food.

On that note, I head over to *The Hungry Gull*.

Waiting in line ahead of me, a couple holds hands, and the woman has a book tucked under her arm—the same one I read last month. When she turns and offers a smile, I can't help but comment.

"*The Whispered Secret?* I just finished that one." I gesture to the book.

She flips the cover around. "Oh, you've read it too? I'm Rachel, by the way, and this is Grant."

"Alex."

"-andra Sinclair? The food writer everyone is talking about?" she teases, and Grant smiles indulgently at her.

"The very one."

"I wouldn't have guessed a famous journalist would read smutty thrillers."

I shrug. "Sorry to break the illusion, but I'm just a regular person like everyone else."

Her responding laughter is warm. "So, what did you think of the twist in the middle? I didn't see it coming at all."

"Me either, but the way the author wove in the clues was brilliant."

"I know, right? I was up half the night! Our book club talked about it for over an hour."

A woman walks up and announces that a table is available. "Well, nice to meet you, Alex! Enjoy your dinner!"

"You too."

Once I get a seat in the bustling diner, I order the pie

mentioned in the brochure. The owner sits me in a vinyl booth where the cracked red seat squeaks every time I shift. The linoleum floor has seen better days, and the jukebox in the corner looks like it's been here since the '50s.

But none of that matters when I find myself staring at a slice of cherry pie that looks like it belongs in a food stylist's dream portfolio.

The crust is golden and flaky, the lattice top so beautiful it practically makes my inner perfectionist swoon. Steam rises from the filling, carrying the intoxicating scent of ripe cherries and warm spices. It's the kind of pie that would have culinary school instructors wiping away tears of joy.

And that's the problem.

I take a bite, and the flavors explode on my tongue. The cherries burst with sweetness, their tart edge perfectly balancing the rich, buttery crust that melts in my mouth. For a moment, I swear I can taste sunshine, laughter, and the pure bliss of a summer day. Which, I know, is ridiculous. Those aren't even flavors.

I set my fork down, a frown tugging at my lips. How is a greasy spoon diner in the middle of nowhere serving pies that could rival those from the world's finest bakeries? Where are they getting these impossibly fresh ingredients? And why isn't there a line out the door for this culinary miracle? The place is no busier than any other quiet night in a small town.

"Everything all right, honey?" Hazel asks, appearing at my elbow with a coffee pot. Her gray hair is piled high on her head, and grease splatters her apron.

"It's delicious," I say, because it is. "I just... how do you do it?"

Hazel winks, the wrinkles around her eyes crinkling. "Family secret. Can't go spilling that to a big-city reporter, now can I?"

As she walks away, I could swear I see a shimmer in the air

around her, like a desert mirage. I rub my eyes, the world blurring for a moment before snapping back into focus.

The late nights must be getting to me.

What time I haven't spent working on other articles, I've used the excruciatingly slow internet at the bed and breakfast to search for answers... about *anything*.

About Magnolia Cove. *(Which barely exists outside of Ethan's bakery.)* About Ethan. *(Who barely exists outside mentions of The Whimsical Whisk.)* About everything on this island that doesn't make sense.

It's a wonder this place has even made it onto the Clip-Clop app, much less gone viral. People must take videos and post them when they're back on the mainland, because there's not enough internet in every shop combined to do that from Magnolia Cove.

I've even shot off an email to another journalist asking for help with research.

There's just something about this place that doesn't quite add up.

There's something about Ethan that doesn't make sense.

I'm probably staying up so late working because if I try to sleep, my mind goes to him.

To his gigantic smile and the way he bows his head if he's praised.

To the teasing but clearly affectionate relationship between him and Zoe.

To him discussing how he gained his passion for baking at his grandmother's side, then refined it by charming Parisian neighbors and working his way into their kitchens with his broken French and overly eager manners—both of which they scolded.

I'm smiling again, and someone sitting at the counter looks my way. I clear my throat and finish my pie, savoring every bite even as I don't understand it.

The rest of the day passes in a blur of interviews and note-taking, each conversation leaving me with more questions than answers. I chat with Tom Bryson, the owner of the bait and tackle shop, who swears the fish practically jump into your boat here. He spends a solid five minutes trying to charm me into taking one of his fishing tours—dropping phrases like *once-in-a-lifetime experience* and *you haven't lived until you've reeled in a redfish at sunrise.* I politely decline, but he just grins and tells me I'll change my mind before I leave town.

Then there's the florist, who hides behind her desk, glaring at the sun streaming through the window but insists that her blooms last twice as long as others. And the surly teenager working at the museum? He just shrugs off my questions when the exhibits offer no more information than the books I bought.

By the time evening rolls around, my head is spinning, my notebook is full of useless notes, and my stomach is rumbling. My feet carry me to *The Whimsical Whisk* almost of their own accord, drawn by the promise of Ethan's warm smile and the comforting scent of fresh-baked bread.

The *Closed* sign is up, but lights still gleam inside. For a moment, I hesitate. I shouldn't bother them after hours. I'm about to turn away when Zoe appears at the door, grinning like the Cheshire Cat.

"Well, well, if it isn't our favorite foodie," she says, opening the door. Flour dusts her hair, fading her purple streaks to lilac. "Come to uncover more of our nefarious baking secrets?"

"I was just hoping for a quiet place to work, actually. But if you're closed—"

"Nonsense." Zoe waves a hand dismissively, nearly smacking me with the dish towel she's holding. "Mi bakery es su bakery. Ethan's in the back with the kid. I'm sure he won't mind if you set up shop out here."

Before I can protest, she ushers me inside. The bakery is quiet, the display cases empty save for a few lonely muffins. Lingering scents of the day's baking hang thick in the air—cinnamon, vanilla, and something deeper, richer, that I can't quite place.

"I'm heading out, but stay as long as you like," Zoe says, grabbing her jacket from a hook. "Just don't go snooping in the secret ingredient cabinet. That's where we keep all the magic." She winks at me, then calls out, "Ethan! Your girl-friend's here!"

I splutter, heat rushing to my face. "Oh, that's not why I'm here... we're not—"

But Zoe's already out the door, her laughter floating back on the evening breeze.

Ethan appears from the kitchen, a flour-dusted apron tied around his waist. It reminds me of the *Foodie Frenzy* photo where he'd posed in a perfectly starched apron—one I haven't seen that clean since I got here. His curls are more jumbled than usual, and when he smiles, dimples crease his cheeks. My heart definitely doesn't skip a beat at the sight. Nope. Not at all.

"Alex. Everything okay?"

"I'm so sorry." I clutch my laptop bag like a lifeline. "Zoe let me in, but I can go if—"

"No, no," he cuts me off with a wave that sends another dusting of flour into the air. "You're welcome to stay. I'm just working with a friend on a new recipe. Set up out here if you want."

Relief washes over me. My room hasn't been great for working, and I feel peaceful at the Whisk. It's a feeling that keeps drawing me back. "Thanks. I promise I won't get under your feet like I did in our disastrous meeting."

His eyes crinkle at the corners. "I believe I ran into *you* with that tray of pastries, not the other way around."

"We'll have to agree to disagree on that, Chief."

He laughs, and as he disappears back into the kitchen, I settle at a table, spreading out my notes and opening my laptop. The keys clack loudly in the quiet room as I type up my observations from the day. But instead of focusing on my work, I find myself straining to hear the conversation from the kitchen.

"Okay, Jas," Ethan's voice carries through. "Now we need to temper the chocolate. This is tricky, but I know you can do it."

"I don't know," a younger voice responds, uncertainty clear in his tone. "What if I mess it up?"

"Then we'll start over," Ethan says simply. "That's the beauty of baking. There's always a chance to try again."

There's a pause, filled with the sound of whisks against metal bowls. Then Jas speaks again, his voice smaller. "Do you think I'll ever be as good as you?"

"I think you'll be better," Ethan replies without hesitation. "You've got a natural talent, kiddo."

"Tell that to the kids at school," Jas mutters. "They all think I'm weird for liking baking. Say I should play sports like my brothers."

Missy comes to mind at his words. The grim years after our parents' loss, when music was the only thing that kept her from drowning. Her passion set her apart, made her the odd one out in a sea of kids more interested in sports and social media. She'd come home in the afternoons, cello case dragging behind her, eyes red-rimmed from holding back tears.

She persevered, though, and now she's at Juilliard, living her dream. A dream that's come with a hefty price tag. Soon she'll be in Paris, honing her skills under the guidance of masters in buildings older than the city we live in. It's an incredible opportunity, one that could launch her career, but the cost...

I shake my head, trying to focus on the present. That's why I've come to Magnolia Cove. It's not just about advancing my career or writing groundbreaking exposés. It's about making sure Missy gets her chance to shine after life tried to drag her down.

That's why, despite the Whisk and its owner's charm, I have to stay focused. I need to nail this article, uncover whatever is going on in Magnolia Cove, and return home with my and Missy's futures firmly secured.

"Hey," Ethan's voice from the back room is gentle but firm, cutting through my thoughts like a knife skimming through butter. "There's nothing weird about following your passion. You know, I used to feel different too. Like I didn't quite fit in anywhere."

"Really?" Jas sounds skeptical. "But you're so cool."

Ethan's laughter rings out, warm and genuine. "Trust me, when I was younger, no one would have agreed with you on that. But you know what I learned? Being different, embracing what makes you unique—that's what makes the world beautiful. Just like how different flavors come together to make an amazing dessert."

"I guess," Jas says, sounding a bit more cheerful. "And I bet none of those jerks can make a chocolate soufflé."

"Exactly," Ethan agrees. "Now, let's make this the best darn truffles Magnolia Cove has ever seen."

I'm smiling, warmth spreading through my chest. There's something about Ethan's words, about the gentle way he's guiding *the kid,* as Zoe dubbed him, that makes me see the Whisk's owner in a whole new light. It's more than just his good looks or his baking skills. There's a kindness, a depth to him I hadn't expected.

But as I turn back to my notes, that nagging feeling returns. The pie that tasted of happiness. The shimmer in the air. Ethan's words about making the world beautiful.

What if... what if there really is something magical about this town?

I shake my head, trying to clear it. That's crazy talk. There's no such thing as magic. I'm a journalist, for crying out loud. I deal in facts, in things I can see and touch and prove.

And yet...

I think about the way Ethan's scones seemed to melt my stress away. How Hazel's pie made me *taste* emotions. The way flowers bloom impossibly large and vibrant all over town.

My fingers hover over my keyboard as I debate what to write. The rational part of my brain says to stick to the facts— the recipes, the techniques, the local color.

But another part, a part I'm not entirely comfortable acknowledging, wants to dive into the mystery. To explore the possibility that there's more to Magnolia Cove than meets the eye. It's not something *Gastronomy Eats* would ever buy. We deal in hard facts, true stories, and reliable recipe techniques. Yet, for the first time in my life, I'm drawn to something that seems more fiction than reality.

The air in the bakery feels charged, as if the very molecules are vibrating with an energy I can't explain. I think of the inexplicable comfort of Ethan's pastries, the way Zoe's grin seems to sparkle with hidden knowledge, the peculiar phrases that slip out when the locals don't think I'm listening. There's a story here, one that defies the rigid boundaries of food journalism.

In the kitchen, Ethan and Jas laugh. The sound echoes through the Whisk, matching the space. Everything about the bakery—the island—feels like coming home after a long, miserable trip.

I stretch my fingers, then begin to type.

Magnolia Cove is a town of secrets, of flavors that can't be described and sights that defy explanation. It's a place where pies taste of summer days and scones can lift your spirits. Where a bear of a man teaches a young boy that being different is beautiful, and where a jaded city journalist might just start to believe in magic...

I pause, my finger hovering over the backspace key. It's not my usual style. It's not the lush descriptions and sharp facts I usually write. But as I read over the words, my grin lingers.

I save the document, making sure I won't lose my words. I'm uncertain anyone else will ever see them, but for some reason, I want to hold on to the story. Hold on to the experience. For now, I'm content to sit in this quiet bakery, listening to the sound of childhood giggles and the whisper of something that feels like magic in the air. Then, before fate—or Magnolia Cove—can throw another ridiculously charming local in my path, I snap my laptop shut, grab my things, and head out, leaving Ethan to mentor his young apprentice in peace.

Ethan

The evening light filters through the bakery windows, painting everything in soft, golden hues. It's the kind of light that makes even day-old muffins look magazine-worthy. I'm wiping down the counters, lost in thought, when Alex's voice cuts through my reverie.

"Hey, Ethan? Can I ask you something?"

I look up, my heart doing that annoying little skip it does whenever I see her. She leans against the display case, notebook in hand, strands of hair fallen loose from her updo. I have to resist the urge to brush them away. There's something elegant about her—something that makes her stand out against the laid-back, coastal vibes of everyone else here.

"Sure," I say, trying to keep my voice casual. "What's up?"

She takes a deep breath, like she's steeling herself. "I was wondering if I could work as an apprentice with you for the week. You know, to learn more about your baking techniques and take some pictures for the article. I'm really intrigued by the Whisk's unique approach to baking. There's something special about your pastries, something I can't put my finger on. I'd love to get a behind-the-scenes look and really understand what makes this place distinct."

The rag slips from my hand, landing with a wet splat on the floor. "You want to... apprentice?"

A jolt rushes through me. On one hand, working closely together would be the perfect opportunity to show her the heart of The Whimsical Whisk, to prove we're more than just flashy marketing. On the other hand, keeping our secrets hidden while she's watching our every move? That's a recipe for disaster.

Alex nods, her eyes brightening. "It would be great for the story. Plus, I'd love to learn from you. Your baking is..." A faint blush colors her cheeks. "Well, it's kind of magical."

Magical. The word echoes in my head, setting off alarm bells. I can almost hear Dean's gravelly voice warning me about exposure, about the risks of getting too close. Telling me I needed to get Alex to leave as quickly as possible.

"I... I don't know," I stammer. I bend down and grab the rag just to have something to do with my hands. "It's a busy time with the season picking up, and I already have Jasper coming in the afternoons three times a week."

"Oh." The disappointment in her voice is like a punch to the gut. "I understand. I just thought..."

"It's not that I don't want to," I say quickly, hating the way her face falls. "It's just... complicated. I'll need to think through the logistics."

She nods, but I can see the questions forming behind her eyes. Questions I can't answer without putting everything at risk.

"Maybe we can revisit the idea tomorrow?" I offer, grasping at straws.

Alex's smile doesn't quite reach her eyes. "Sure, of course. Thanks anyway, Ethan."

As she gathers her things to leave, I feel like I'm watching something precious slip through my fingers.

But what choice do I have?

The bakery feels emptier than usual after she's gone. I go through the motions of closing up, my mind a whirlwind of conflicting thoughts and emotions.

Zoe finds me like this, staring blankly at the day's receipts.

"Earth to Ethan," she says, waving a hand in front of my face. "You planning on sleeping here or what?"

I blink, coming back to myself. "Sorry, just... lost in thought."

She eyes me suspiciously. "Uh-huh. And would those thoughts happen to involve a certain food writer? The one you can't seem to keep your focus off even when you're elbow-deep in bread dough? I swear, Sugar, you're gonna end up with a face full of flour if you keep swiveling your head every time she walks by."

I groan, dropping my head into my hands. "Am I that obvious?"

It's more than just Alex's polished beauty that draws me in —it's the way she brightens when she talks about restaurants she's visited, the chefs she's interviewed, the cities she's explored. Every story is like a window into a world I can't access, not while I'm bound to Magnolia Cove and Dean Markham's watchful eye. She speaks of pop-up stalls in Chelsea serving hand-pulled noodles with the same excitement she uses to describe the fresh-picked flowers placed daily on wobbly tables in a hidden café in Prague.

Alex represents everything I can't have: a life lived beyond these shores and a love that doesn't require hiding who—and what—I really am.

"Of all your skills, lying isn't one of them. You're about as subtle as one of your triple chocolate cakes. It's part of your charm." Zoe pats my shoulder. "Come on, I'll walk you home. Looks like you could use some fresh air."

The evening is crisp and salty as we step outside. The streetlights cast a warm glow over the cobblestone, making Main Street gleam. In the distance, waves lap against the shore, the sound echoing down to us. A few lingering tourists stroll along the sidewalks, their laughter carrying on the breeze.

As we walk, I tell Zoe about Alex's request, about my panic, about the weight of responsibility I feel.

"Am I crazy for regretting not accepting her proposition immediately? I mean, this could be our big break." We turn onto the beach path, and a seagull scuttles off before flying into the darkening sky. "After what happened last time..."

"Last time was different," Zoe says firmly. An unusual darkness enters her eyes. She was one of the first people to befriend me in the Cove when I'd arrived—heartbroken, angry. Afraid I'd lost everything I'd ever worked for. She was the one who made me believe in starting the Whisk. "You've learned and grown. And Alex isn't Sarah."

I stuff my hands into my pockets. Sarah, the human girl I fell for years ago. The one who discovered my secret, who reacted with terror, who almost exposed our whole community. The memory of her wide, frightened eyes and the sound of her screams still haunt me—a stark reminder of why I need to be so careful. Why I can't let myself get too close to anyone else.

We reach the hill's crest, and the full beauty of the island spreads out before us. The moon is rising, a perfect silver disc reflected in the calm waters of the bay. To our right, hidden from human eyes, is the shimmer of the barrier that protects our magical sanctuary.

"It's nights like these that remind me how precious this place is," I say softly. "How much we have to lose if I screw up again."

Zoe stops walking, turning to face me. "Hey, Boss, what-ever catastrophe you're cooking up in that flour-filled brain of yours? It's not as bad as you think."

I raise an eyebrow. "No? Because from where I'm stand-ing, it looks like I'm risking everything our people have built here. Again. All because I... because I..."

"Because you like her," Zoe finishes for me. "News flash, Ethan: liking someone isn't a crime."

"It is when you're someone like me," I mutter. "Even in our world, I'm... different. Dangerous. And she's a human journalist who could expose everything. Maybe Dane has a point."

Zoe rolls her eyes. "Oh please. You're not the big bad wolf —you're a teddy bear with imposter syndrome who happens to make the best damn pastries this side of the Pacific Ocean." She smirks before continuing, "And if you're actually consid-ering Dean's opinion, I'm worried you've been huffing too much of that special vanilla extract you ordered."

Despite myself, a smile tugs at my lips. "That vanilla is too expensive to use for anything we don't make a profit on. Besides, you're biased."

"Damn straight I am," she says, grinning. "Look, I get why you're scared. But you can't live your whole life in fear of what might happen."

We start walking again, the waves growing louder as our feet meet the shore. We're both lucky to live in resident cottages overlooking the sea. The sickeningly sweet scent of night-blooming jasmine somehow feels right, tangling with the ocean breeze.

"I just... I have responsibilities," I say. "To Jasper, to the town, to our people. I can't risk all that for... what? A fleeting feeling?"

Zoe snorts. "A fleeting feeling? Please. I've seen the way you look at her, Ethan. It's more than that, and you know it."

I open my mouth to argue, but she cuts me off. "And before you go all noble sacrifice on me, consider this: maybe letting her in, even just a little, is exactly what you both need."

She shrugs. "I mean, okay, so maybe you can't tell her everything. But you can let her apprentice. Show her the non-magical side of baking. Who knows? Maybe it'll satisfy her curiosity enough that she stops digging. And maybe she'll write an honest piece about how damn amazing your creations are. You might use magic to infuse good feelings into them, but the technique is all you, Boss."

We round the bend, where the cottage lights glow warmly in the distance. "You really think that could work?"

"I think it's worth a shot. I can distract her. You have no idea just how much chaos I can cook up in a pinch." Zoe bumps her shoulder against my arm, and I chuckle. "Besides, I believe in love and magic. It's not just a line we feed the tourists, you know."

As if on cue, Mia turns the corner, a book tucked under her arm. A grin spreads across Zoe's face.

"Speaking of that," she says, quickening her pace. She throws an arm around Mia's neck and presses a kiss to her cheek. "Hey, babe. Ready to head home?"

Mia clasps the hand slung over her shoulder and smiles.

"Night, Ethan," Zoe calls as they turn to leave. "Try not to overthink things, okay?"

I wave, watching as they walk away, heads bent close in quiet conversation. Something aches in my chest. I'm never going to have what they do—someone to come home to, someone who knows and accepts all of me, who loves me despite it.

The moon is high now, bathing everything in silver light. I take a deep breath, letting the familiar scents and sounds of the island wash over me. This place is magic, yes, but it's also become home. Maybe, if I'm careful, it might be the launching pad to help make some of my dreams come true—to be more than just a small-town baker, to make a mark on the culinary world.

I think about Alex's hopeful face when she asked to apprentice, about the way she gestures with her hands as she discusses food. I think about Zoe's words—about taking risks and believing in possibilities.

Maybe I can't give Alex everything. Maybe I can't answer the questions she really wants to ask or return anything more than smiles. But I can give her this—a week in my kitchen, a glimpse into my world. That's what she loves to write about anyway.

Alex Sinclair isn't looking for magic—not the kind we're trying to hide. She's looking for the passion behind food stories, the people who sacrifice and spend excruciating years perfecting their craft.

That, I can show her.

It wasn't magic that made me a baker but years of studying. Leaving home and traveling to France. Having my knuckles cracked by the back of wooden spoons and spending every penny I made on T55 flour and fleur de sel so I could practice with my unreliable oven until I perfected a recipe.

As I turn toward home, I feel something settle in my chest. A decision, yes, but also a spark of something that feels dangerously like hope.

Tomorrow, I'll tell Alex she can apprentice. I'll keep my powers under wraps, stick to the non-magical side of baking. And maybe, just maybe, I'll let myself enjoy having her around.

As long as I stick to that, nothing could go wrong. Possibly, she'll even write an article that might open me up to new opportunities when I've finished paying off my time in Magnolia Cove. Maybe I'll actually escape my past.

The thought carries me home, a smile on my face and the taste of possibility sweet on my tongue.

Alex

The Whisk has a lone light gleaming from somewhere in the back, but it otherwise appears as sleepy and closed up as the shops surrounding it. I clutch the handle and hesitate. When it pulls open without resistance, the bell tinkling into the early morning quiet, I startle.

Typical small-town attitude—not worrying about locking up. I'm starting to wonder if Zoe was right about her fungal growth comment, because every day I spend in Magnolia Cove, I want to spend another. Every moment I'm parked behind my computer screen, the salty breeze, people's laughter, and savory restaurant smells beckon me.

"Hello?" I call into the dark of the Whisk's dining room. Even in the shadows, there's something homey about the space. It reminds me of waking up on Christmas morning, clambering down to the living room before the lights are on, but knowing soon all will glow and smell of good things and sound like laughter. "Ethan?"

It surprised me when, after thinking things through, he said I could apprentice for the week. There's something he's hiding, but I can't figure out what it is. His recipes are top-notch, his connection with the community seems as golden as *Food Frenzy* magazine made it sound. Yet his eyes dart away at innocuous questions, and there's a trace of unease in our interactions that feels out of place.

"Back here!" Ethan pops his head out of the kitchen and smiles. It reminds me of my conversation with Missy the day before.

So, is the baker as cute as he seems on ClipClop?

I'd rolled my eyes and shot back that she was trying to distract me from asking about her finals. But I'd swirled that question around in my mind all night. Now, as he takes a step forward, his T-shirt cuffs tight around his biceps, his sandy curls tumbling across his brow, I realize I was the one deflecting. Because, yes, Ethan Hart is every bit as gorgeous as he appeared in the fifteen-second videos or in the glossy magazine spread.

"I brought coffee." I lift the to-go cups as I step with him into the kitchen.

He accepts a cup but sniffs it, his lips thinning like he's fighting a grimace.

"Not a fan of coffee?"

"Um... I like coffee."

I walk behind the counter with him, past the kitchen island where they prepare things during customer hours, and toward the glowing light of the back room. "Something wrong with this coffee, Chief?"

He looks back at me, offering a lopsided grin that makes my heart tumble, though I'd deny it to Missy and Tish forever.

"You picked that up at Hazel's, didn't you?"

The cups' warmth has seeped into my hands, and suddenly, I feel a bizarre need to defend Hazel and her little run-down diner. "She makes excellent pie."

"She does." He nods and crosses his arms, stretching his shirt over his muscled chest, which makes it very difficult to focus on my completely illogical desire to defend a woman I've met precisely three times in my life. Then Ethan smirks. "But the magic ends there. Her coffee is terrible."

I open my mouth to argue, but he shakes his head. "Try a taste, then tell me what you think."

I lift the cup and breathe it in—then freeze, struggling not to cough. Ethan's grin only widens, making me want to slap the cups down until they slosh over his spotless countertops. Jutting up my chin, I take the smallest sip. The burnt, bitter flavor floods my mouth, and I fight every muscle in my face to keep my expression neutral. The twinkle in Ethan's eye says I've failed miserably.

"It's all right," he says. "I keep a pot of the good stuff back here."

He sweeps his arm toward the kitchen, then offers to take the horrible coffee. I gladly hand it off. I'd rather go through the day in a caffeine-free haze than take another sip of Hazel's coffee.

"Here we are," Ethan says. "The heart of the Whisk."

A breath rushes past my lips as I take in the kitchen. If I had any lingering doubts that Ethan was the real deal, this wood-countertop-laden, well-lit kitchen would dispel them.

An entire wall of shelves lines one side near the fridge. Jars with handwritten labels fill them. There are a dozen flours— whole wheat, almond, spelt, rye, and more. Below that shelf sit half a dozen jars of sugar, including demerara and pearl sugar, followed by mix-ins like cranberries and cocoa nibs.

In another corner, a large metal planter sits below a heat lamp, herbs growing happily under the golden light. A shelf to the right holds cookbooks crammed together like a game of Tetris, their pages decorated with bookmarks, tabs, and food splatters.

There are enough baking pans and spatulas back here to keep a full team busy through the busiest holiday rush, yet the only employees I've seen at the Whisk so far are Ethan, Zoe, and a handful of local teenagers who run the cash register in the afternoons.

It's eclectic and cozy and smells like creamed butter and sugar. It reminds me—I realize with a start—of my apartment's kitchen back home. The stacks of books, the trio of overstuffed spoon holders. The variety of ingredients, a testament to someone who truly loves the craft.

For a moment, I'm somewhere else entirely. Back in my tiny kitchen, late at night, exhaustion settled deep in my bones, but Missy insisting we make cookies anyway. *Mom never measured,* she'd said, dumping a reckless amount of vanilla into the batter. *She just knew.* We'd ended up with a tray of the sweetest, messiest cookies imaginable, eating them straight from the parchment paper, burnt edges and all.

A lump forms in my throat, unexpected and unwelcome. This space, this feeling—it's home. And I don't know what to do with that.

Ethan watches me take in the space, his forehead furrowed. He's worried that I might find his bakery wanting, that I'll decide he falls short. That I'll print it publicly for the world to read. Erase any credibility he might ever hope to gain.

Which is exactly what I'm here to do.

To my right, a dozen glass jars of sourdough starters are pushed against the back wall, each labeled in Sharpie with various clever names. Doughy Parton sits next to Sir Rise-a-Lot, and at the very end, a particularly bubbly batch bears the label Bread Sheeran.

"Cute names," I say as Ethan hands me a mug of coffee. I take a deep breath and close my eyes, savoring the aroma. Now this is excellent coffee—warm, bold, and with just the right hint of something nutty.

He hides his face behind his own mug. "Zoe named them."

"What are we working on today?"

He takes another sip, then sets his mug down. "Lavender cake to start—a special order for Mrs. Delehay's bridge club. In an hour, when Zoe comes in, we'll get the morning pastries going and start prep for the lunch crowd."

He offers me an apron, and I loop it over my head and tie it on. The motion is comforting—familiar. Being awake before the rest of the world, the whir of ovens warming, the quiet hum of the kitchen—this is a rhythm I know.

Ethan pulls down a mixing bowl, setting it on the counter with a soft thump. He gathers ingredients, including a jar of dried lavender buds.

"Lavender cake is a very specific order," I say.

Ethan's grin reminds me of the picture of him in *Food Frenzy*. Except I realize what I mistook for artificial was actually discomfort. Now, his smile is broad, wrinkling his eyes, accompanied by a soft sigh. "Mrs. Delehay keeps thinking she'll trip me up one of these days. Every week, she orders something different—and always at the last minute. The postmaster told me she started subscribing to food magazines just to keep me on my toes."

He walks over to the fridge and comes back with a glass bottle of milk, setting it on the counter. Unscrewing the cap, he reaches for a measuring cup and pours, his movements precise. I step a little closer, curious despite myself, watching as he transfers the measured milk into a saucepan.

My arms cross. "The postmaster told you about a resident's private mail?"

He huffs a laugh. "Small towns."

"You've lived in several bigger cities if I'm right? You've mentioned that Parisian baking influenced your approach?"

He turns away to open a jar of dried lavender. I lean in slightly, watching as he shakes some into the pan. The soft floral scent curls into the air between us as he stirs slowly, then gives a one-word answer.

"Yes."

Okay, then. My journalist brain is burning, my hand itching for a pen, but there's something delicate in Ethan's eyes when he meets my gaze—something that makes my breath catch.

He turns the pot down to a simmer and moves to the mixer. I take another step, drawn to the rhythmic motion of sugar and butter whipping together.

"What inspired you to move to a small town, then? The beach? The opportunity to bring big-city flavor to a niche audience?"

"Yeah." His voice is raspy, and he won't meet my eyes. More lies. But they feel like gentle half-truths, like telling a kid that Santa Claus is real.

I lift my chin, realizing too late just how close we've gotten. *Too close.* The heat of him radiates against my skin, and for a ridiculous second, I think about how easily he could drop his head and brush a kiss against my nose.

My heart leaps by the time he speaks again. "I suppose you've never felt trapped by your circumstances before?"

A laugh—bitter-edged—spills out of me. "Only every single day."

He turns the mixer off and frowns at me. His eyes trace over my face like he's seeking answers himself. I've never been on this side of an interview. I always hide behind my laptop, behind my professional merit. *Alexandra Sinclair* is a name splashed across matte-covered magazines—but never accompanied by a picture. Never anything personal.

It feels like too much. *Too close.*

"What has you trapped, then?"

I turn and grab the carton of eggs, then hold them out toward him.

Ethan doesn't take them straight away. Instead, he continues to look at me in a way no one ever has—intense, unguarded, like he's seeing right through all my defenses.

Our breathing fills the air between us. The bakery is so quiet—nothing more than the hum of ovens, the milk's quiet simmer. Each breath tastes like vanilla. Ethan's gaze drops to my lips, then back to my eyes. My breath hitches, and the urge to lean in and find out if he *tastes* like the vanilla-scented air becomes unbearable.

I'm going to become the most unprofessional journalist that's ever existed. I'm going to kiss the firefighter-calendar-look-alike baker at 3:30 a.m. in his bakery in this magical little town, and he's going to taste like sugar.

"My dad's here, in Magnolia Cove."

Ethan accepts the eggs and turns from me, breaking the moment.

I let out a shaky breath. *What the hell is happening to me?* I'm going to get myself fired. I'm not sure what spell this little town and this gorgeous man have cast on me, but I need to finish out this week, get my answers, and get out of here.

Ethan cracks the eggs into a small bowl, then blends them in smoothly. He grabs a whiskey bottle and pours a generous splash of what must be homemade vanilla. The scent is so intoxicatingly rich I take a long breath, letting the aroma fill my senses. It's warm and layered, with hints of caramel and oak—almost tempting enough to taste on its own.

"The circumstance that's keeping me stuck," I whisper, "is family too."

Ethan turns back to me. I never understood what people meant when they said someone appeared haunted, but I do now. Ethan's eyes have gone dark, his forehead furrowed.

The mixer is whirring on unsupervised, and for a fleeting moment, I think this might be the dessert Mrs. Delehay finally gets to boast about—beating Ethan Hart's abilities. Because with the way he's looking at me, I won't remind him he might overwhip the batter. That he should check the milk.

No, I'm going to kiss him, run my hands over his muscular chest, rake my fingers through his curls, and end up fired for unprofessional behavior—and I don't even care.

"Taking care of parents?" he asks, his voice low and rumbling. The sound of it does strange things to my insides.

"A younger sister, actually."

"Ah."

He takes a step closer to me. I was wrong to think Ethan smelled only of the pastries he spends his days creating. That's there, like a coat he wears, but beneath it, there's something warmer—earthy, like cedarwood.

I tilt my chin up, because *forget* my career, forget the lavender cake, forget photographing, forget writing, even. All I want is his mouth on mine, his broad hand gliding along my neck, his—

"Hola, good morning, Boss."

Zoe walks in through the back door and is halfway to hanging her jacket on a hook when she stops to stare at both of us.

"Sorry. Did I interrupt something?"

"No," Ethan and I both say together so quickly that it's clear the answer is yes.

Zoe purses her lips until they pop, then turns and grabs her apron. "Okay, then."

I step back, my heart hammering against my ribs. The loss of his nearness feels like stepping from sunlight into shade.

"I should take a couple of pictures," I say before turning toward where I'd dropped my camera bag. My fingers tremble. Ugh. Damn me for getting so flustered over this man. I don't get flustered. I ask sharp questions, take meticulous notes, and keep my emotions in check. Even if he is six feet of gorgeous baker with eyes that remind me of summer skies.

Zoe gives her hips a little shimmy. "I have a playlist that's going to knock your socks off this morning, Boss, City Girl."

"City Girl?" I lift my face from behind the camera. Ethan has returned to the simmering milk, but he groans loudly enough for it to reach us.

"Ignore him," Zoe whispers to me. "He won't tell you this, but he hired me because I'm the fun half of the Whisk. Didn't know a thing about baking when we started the place."

I chuckle just as Zoe slips her phone out and starts blasting Earth, Wind & Fire through speakers I hadn't noticed before.

How did Zoe and Ethan start the Whisk together? Why would he choose someone who had no baking experience? And how did he end up in Magnolia Cove of all places?

Throughout the morning, Ethan and Zoe act in perfect synchronization, like dancers who've rehearsed the steps a thousand times. He doesn't even look up when she slides a bowl of something that smells like cinnamon and sunshine to him. For someone who supposedly taught her everything about baking in the last three years, their rhythm feels very... practiced.

And Magnolia Cove itself. I've visited dozens of small coastal towns for the magazine, but none of them feel quite like this. None of them have air that sometimes seems to sparkle, or shadows that move when they shouldn't, or baked goods that taste like memories feel.

My camera captures Ethan as he pipes delicate swirls onto the lavender cake. His hands never hesitate, never falter. Like magic, I think, then I almost laugh at myself. There's a perfectly reasonable explanation for all of this. There has to be.

Doesn't there?

Ethan

Running a bakery while hiding magic from a particularly observant food writer is a lot like trying to frost a wedding cake in an earthquake. Technically possible, but likely to end in disaster.

I should have said no when Alex asked to apprentice for the week. Dean would have wanted me to. But the memory of her lips nearly brushing mine, of her body heat radiating against my skin, of vanilla perfume mingling with rising dough—it haunts me. The wanting sits deep in my bones, an ache I can't shake. Alex Sinclair looks at me like I'm something special, like I'm more than just magic and secrets and shame. Like I'm someone worth knowing.

And that's exactly why I should have turned her away. Because the more time she spends here, watching me with those keen eyes that miss nothing, the harder it becomes to remember all the reasons I can't have this. Can't have her.

"Quick, distract her!" I hiss at Zoe as Alex's footsteps echo down the hallway. My hands hum with magic as I infuse comfort into a batch of chocolate chip cookies. We can't let Alex see the shimmer.

Zoe springs into action, practically throwing herself into Alex's path. "Oh my god, did I ever tell you about the time I accidentally dyed one of our sourdough starters blue?" It's completely made up—we'd never risk the precious starters—but Alex doesn't know that. She pauses in the doorway, note-book in hand. I make use of the time, infusing as much magic as I can.

"And that's why we had to rename Sir Rise-a-Lot to Blues Clues for an entire month," Zoe finishes with a dramatic flourish.

Alex laughs, the sound warming me more than any magic could. She's been here for days now, watching us work, taking notes, asking questions. Her presence is intoxicating and terri-fying in equal measure. Every time she walks into a room, my magic hums beneath my skin, eager to show off. To show her everything.

But I can't. Even if the Council hadn't strictly forbidden it, the memory of Sarah's screams still haunts me. The way her eyes had widened in horror, how she'd backed away...

"Earth to Ethan!" Zoe's voice snaps me back to the present. "The cookies?"

I blink down at them. Right. The magic is settled now, infused into the cookies, impossible to distinguish from any other batch. I scoop them onto a cooling rack just as Alex steps fully into the kitchen, flipping to a fresh page in her notebook.

"Smells incredible," she says, eyes bright. "What's next?"

I barely get my mouth open before Zoe, flour-dusted and absolutely up to something, claps her hands together. "Ethan's about to teach you the recipe."

I pause. "What?"

Alex raises an eyebrow. "Go on."

Zoe grins. "You know, the recipe. The one every customer begs for. The one that makes people emotional. The one that, if he ever revealed it, would surely get him burned at the stake for crimes against baked goods." She leans in conspiratorially. "The Whimsical Whisk's world-famous, to-die-for cinnamon rolls."

Alex's lips part slightly. "You'd really show me that one?"

Before I can interject, Zoe gasps. "Only if you swear— cross your heart, hope to die—that you'll keep the magic a secret."

The words land heavier than they should. It's a joke, obviously. She isn't actually asking Alex to keep real magic secret. But the way my heart kicks up, the way Alex tilts her head just slightly, like she's weighing something bigger than a simple playful promise—I feel it.

She presses a hand to her chest, eyes locked on mine. "Your secret's safe with me."

I wish that were true.

I swallow hard, nodding once, and move to grab the flour, needing something—anything—to keep my hands busy. Zoe, of course, senses the shift immediately.

She slaps her palms down on the counter. "And I will be making sure Ethan doesn't get too in his feelings about it."

Alex laughs. "Is he one to get sentimental over cinnamon rolls?"

"Sweetheart, of course he is." Zoe tosses me a wicked grin. "It's the man's love language."

I shake my head, willing my pulse to slow. "Are we baking or talking?"

Zoe rolls her eyes. "Both, obviously. Multitasking is what separates us from the animals, Boss."

Alex ties on an apron. "Well, let's get to it then. I'm ready for your life-changing secrets."

"You might find yourself disappointed," I say.

Because the truth is, I have more than one secret. And Alex is dangerously close to unraveling them all.

I've shared this recipe only once before—with Zoe—and that was only because she needed it to help run the bakery. But there's something about Alex that makes me want to open up, to reveal parts of myself I've kept buried deep. Somehow, Zoe knew that before I even realized it. She's always had this uncanny ability to see through me, to nudge me toward things I'm too damn stubborn to admit I even want.

"The secret," I say, measuring flour with practiced motions, "is brown butter and a touch of orange zest. The butter adds depth, makes the cinnamon sing, and the zest gives just enough brightness to make people crave another bite without knowing why."

Alex nods, already jotting notes. "Brown butter for depth, orange zest for brightness—it balances the richness." Her eyes meet mine. "Smart."

"That's our Ethan," Zoe pipes up from where she's pretending to organize supplies. "A regular ol' Einstein—but, you know, with more butter and emotional repression."

I shoot her a look but continue. "The other key is the proofing time. Everyone rushes it, but—"

"The flavor develops in the wait," Alex finishes. Her fingers brush mine as she reaches for the yeast, and warmth spreads up my arm at the contact. "Like a good sourdough."

"Exactly." My voice comes out rougher than intended. She understands food the way I do—like it's a language all its own.

We move in tandem, instinctive, effortless—like we've done this for years instead of days. She reaches for the brown sugar at the same time I do, our hands meeting in the soft granules.

Neither of us pulls away.

Her fingers brush mine, warm and steady, lingering just a second too long. The air shifts, thickens. My pulse kicks up, my breath catching in my throat. Static hums between us—or maybe it's not static at all. Maybe it's my magic, slipping through the cracks, reaching for her despite my best efforts to contain it.

I should step back. Say something. Do anything but stand here, caught in this moment that feels too fragile, too dangerous.

But I don't.

And neither does she.

"The muscovado sugar is from the Philippines," I say, desperate to focus on something other than how her skin feels against mine.

"Mmm." She leans in, inhaling the rich molasses scent. "Is it worth the import costs?"

"Always." I'm not looking at the sugar anymore. I'm watching the way her hair falls forward, catching the kitchen's golden light.

Alex hums in appreciation, her fingers trailing through the sugar, testing its texture—all the while continuing to graze my hand. "You can tell just by looking at it—it's finer, richer. Holds more depth."

"Exactly." My voice is steady, but inside, I am anything but.

She glances up at me then, and I'm pretty sure we aren't talking about sugar anymore.

Her gaze flickers to my mouth—quick, almost imperceptible—but I feel it.

My grip tightens on the edge of the counter. This is dangerous. She's close enough that I could lean in, just a fraction, and taste to see if cinnamon has dusted her lips. I want to.

The air between us stretches, thick with something unspoken.

Then—

"Wow," Zoe drawls, sauntering past the counter. "Didn't realize we were crafting these rolls by hand-milling every grain of flour. You do make these daily, right, Ethan?" She taps the counter, glancing between us, her smirk as subtle as her tie-dye bandana.

I blink, stepping back. Alex laughs, shaking her head, but her cheeks are flushed with something softer, something unspoken.

Zoe waggles her eyebrows at me as she grabs a mixing bowl, her smirk pure mischief. I exhale slowly, forcing myself to move, to focus, to keep my hands busy with the dough. It should be easy—baking's second nature, a rhythm I don't even have to think about. But with Alex here, watching, laughing, filling up the space like she belongs here, nothing feels simple.

Because it's not all banter and close calls. There are moments—quiet ones, usually in the early morning or late evening—when Alex watches me work with such intensity that I forget to breathe. When she asks questions that hit me in the chest, making me wonder if she can see straight through me.

"Why did you choose baking?" she asks one evening as I'm cleaning up. The last of the teenage hires have gone home, and Zoe's off on a date with Mia. It's just us, the soft hum of the ovens, and the lingering scent of sugar and spice that wraps the room like a warm blanket.

I focus on wiping down the counter, stalling for time. "I told you about my grandmother—"

"No," she interrupts gently. "I mean, why did you stick with it? What makes you pour your heart into every single thing you create?"

The truth rises in my throat, sharp and heavy: Because it's the one thing that's entirely mine. Because even with magic, it takes skill, patience, and love. Because when people taste something I've made, they're tasting my soul—not fearing my power.

Instead, I shrug. "I just like making people happy."

She steps closer, and suddenly the kitchen feels too small. "You're good at it. One of the best I've seen, actually." Her hand lands on my arm, and my skin burns where we connect. "You know that, right?"

I meet her eyes, drowning in their warmth. She's so close I can see the flecks of gold in her irises, count each individual eyelash. My magic surges, wanting to show her exactly what I can do, wanting to lay myself bare before her.

The front bell chimes, shattering the moment. Dean stalks in, his dark eyes taking in our proximity with clear disapproval.

"Ms. Sinclair," he says coolly. "I trust you're finding everything you need for your article?"

Alex straightens, her professional mask sliding into place. "Yes, thank you. I've never been somewhere as magical as Magnolia Cove."

Of all the words in the English language, she had to choose "magical." I can practically feel Dean's tension radiating across the room, his magic sharp and crackling beneath the surface. My own rises in response, a reflex as natural as breathing—a silent challenge, one I have no business issuing. I curl my fingers into fists, forcing it down before it can meet his head-on.

"Magical." Dean's voice could freeze hell itself. His jaw flexes, tension rippling through him before he exhales slowly, smoothing his expression into something civilized. "We're glad you're enjoying your stay."

Alex shifts beside me, her posture just a little stiffer than before. She's not afraid of him, but I can tell—she's thrown. Unsettled. Her fingers tighten around the edge of her notebook, her smile polite but faltering at the edges.

She doesn't know what she did wrong.

"Alex has a call with her editor she needs to make. Right?"

My voice is casual. It's taking everything I've got to keep it that way.

She blinks, still half-distracted by Dean's grating presence. "Oh—yeah, I do."

"You don't want to be late."

She glances between us, that keen journalist's intuition clearly picking up on the undercurrent of tension. For a terrifying moment, I think she might press further. But then she nods and wipes her flour-dusted hands on her apron. "Right. I should get going. See you tomorrow, Ethan."

"Tomorrow."

As soon as she's out the door, the temperature drops several degrees, the air turning crisp, charged. Dean's magic brushes against my skin, controlled but unmistakable—a quiet reminder that, if it ever came down to it, he could snuff mine out like a candle. That he's stronger. That he's the one keeping me here, and not the other way around.

He doesn't speak right away. He doesn't have to. The silence says enough.

I wipe my hands on a towel, keeping my movements easy, casual. If he wants to make a point, I won't be the one to invite it.

"This has gone on long enough," Dean finally says. His voice is quiet but sharp as a blade. "Every day she stays increases the risk."

"She's not a threat—"

"No?" He steps closer, magical energy rolling off him in waves. Sometimes I forget that beneath his leather jacket and stern demeanor, Dean is one of the most powerful warlocks in the country. It's no accident he was chosen as my keeper. "You didn't think Sarah was a threat either, and look how that turned out."

I flinch. "That was different."

"Was it?" His dark eyes bore into mine. "You know what

happens if you slip up again. You know what those secure pocket communities really are."

"Locked-down facilities," I mutter, but even saying the words makes my skin crawl. I'd heard whispers about those places—magical beings trapped behind wards so strong they could barely access their own power. No visitors, no freedom, no chance for a normal life. The Whisk might be my cage, but at least it's one that feels normal. One where I can still create, still make others happy, still feel some sense of purpose.

"No." The word cracks like a whip. "They're prisons, Hart. Places where your entire life is managed, twenty-four hours a day. You can forget baking. Forget having any semblance of a normal life." He pauses, letting that sink in. "I chose to allow you to come to Magnolia Cove because I foolishly believe some people deserve second chances. Don't make me regret that."

I study the man before me—powerful enough to make most magical beings tremble, yet here he is in a sleepy coastal town, supposedly choosing an easy post, a quiet life. But then he took me on, and suddenly, his workload wasn't so easy anymore.

I don't know why he did it. Maybe he saw it as a challenge. Maybe it was a test—for both of us. Either way, we've been stuck with each other ever since.

He's the reason I'm here. The reason I was allowed to open a bakery. The reason Magnolia Cove's magical marketing got approved, even though it could have backfired. Hell, he even let Alex stay when he could have forced her out on day one.

For all his gruffness, for all the resentment I harbor at being watched, I owe him my freedom. Such as it is. The Council had wanted me locked away immediately after the Sarah incident. Dean was the one who suggested Magnolia

Cove instead, who volunteered to keep me in check, to be powerful enough to stop me if needed.

And because of that, I got a chance to build something here—to be more than just my mistakes. To knead dough beside Zoe at sunrise, to watch the town square light up with lanterns on festival nights, to be part of something real. I love this town. I love these people. And the last thing I want is to hurt them.

"I understand," I say finally.

Dean nods once, then turns to leave. At the door, he pauses. "End this, Hart. Before I have to."

After he's gone, I sink onto a stool, head in my hands. The kitchen feels cold, despite the residual warmth from the ovens. All my dreams of making a name for myself in the culinary world, of proving I'm more than just my magic—they seem to mock me now.

The truth is, I'm not just hiding magic from Alex. I'm hiding from myself. From the reality that I'll never be normal, never be safe, never be someone who can love freely without fear of destroying everything around them.

I let myself remember the warmth of Alex's touch, the light in her eyes when she tastes something I've made, the way she makes me feel like maybe, just maybe, I could be worthy of love. Even if I know it's just another beautiful illusion.

Alex

Zoe drops a pan of freshly baked bread loaves onto the counter, then places her hands on her hips and surveys their golden crusts. A smile slips across her face. For someone who is new to baking, she definitely loves it, and despite her playfulness, she takes her job seriously.

It's my last day working at the Whisk, and I can't help the melancholy twinge in me at the thought of not showing up again Monday morning, not donning an apron and pulling eggs from the fridge, not greeting the regular customers, not avoiding my actual job.

Because, if I'm honest, the story isn't going anywhere. Not really. I've spent a week up to my elbows in flour and small-town charm, and every time I sit down to write, my brain comes up blank. What am I supposed to say? That the bakery is too warm, too good, too much like a place I want to belong? That the town I was meant to expose has somehow gotten under my skin?

I could get used to this. It's only a dream, though—unattainable. And Ethan, even more so. Despite me falling asleep every night with his dimpled smile floating through my mind and the warm rumble of his voice sending a shiver down my spine. After the first day, I started arriving with Zoe, preventing us from ending up alone together. Because I apparently can't handle 'alone' with Ethan Hart.

Every conversation we share has me drawing closer to him. Just yesterday, he told me—his grin full of mischief—about the time he tried to impress a date with homemade macarons and ended up with what he called 'colorful hockey pucks.' To this day, he still refuses to make them, claiming they're more trouble than they're worth. Naturally, this led to a passionate debate, with me insisting that a well-made macaron is a masterpiece and him staunchly arguing that flavor should always come first—that no baked good should get by on looks alone. Another day, he paced the kitchen at four o'clock in the morning passionately decrying the use of margarine in baked goods. Zoe only chuckled and started another batch of dough.

"Girl, you sound like you're in love already," Tish had said to me last night, her voice echoing through the bed & breakfast's crackling phone line.

"In love? I barely know him!"

"I mean with the bakery, Alex." A pause filled with static, and my breath caught, keeping me from forming words. Tish laughed. "Into the baker too, huh?"

I didn't know how to respond. How could I explain that Magnolia Cove had wormed its way into my heart, that every day with Ethan made it feel more like home? That his laughter, his quiet dedication, even his passionate diatribes on ingredients (he's given several) have become something I look forward to? How can I explain I feel like I've found the life I was supposed to be living all along?

I wonder if the blue of his eyes will ever fade from my memory or if I'll be eighty, lying down at night and seeing his gaze in my dreams. Of course, he's still keeping secrets from me. But I am with him as well. His secrets are probably something harmless and endearing—like the fact that he stole his cinnamon roll recipe from some French pastry chef. Nothing like the truth I'm holding back.

'Would you like to go to dinner?'—a question I've considered asking all week—doesn't exactly pair well with, 'By the way, I'm actually here to ruin your reputation with a scathing critique of your bakery, mostly because it's too heartwarming for people from cold-blooded cities to take seriously.'

That's why I opt to stay up front, running the cash register today, even though it's my last opportunity to work side-by-side with Ethan. I'm afraid he'll see right through me. Perhaps he's feeling the same because he didn't argue about the arrangement.

I hand a banana muffin to Mrs. Delehay, who has her Pomeranian tucked under her arm. She leans in and whispers, "Do you have any suggestions for a complicated dessert to order from our baker?" Her eyes peer over the sunglasses she hasn't removed. "Don't go telling him I asked you, though."

I can't help my smile. The small-town antics that felt borderline cringey when I first walked off the ferry have grown on me. I tap my finger to my chin, then say, "Ask him to make you a croquembouche."

She mouths the word, then pulls out a notepad and asks me to write it down. I do so, then wave as she leaves. That's a dessert that will awe and impress her but will be simple enough for someone with Ethan's skills to pull together. He'll probably enjoy the change of pace, actually.

The bell dings again, and I smile widely at who's walked in. It's Rachel, the woman I met at *The Hungry Gull* before I realized I should stick with their pies and avoid the coffee.

"Hello," I say.

"Well, hey again." She grins. "I heard you'd taken on a job at the Whisk."

"Oh, I'm just observing for the week. Today's my last day,

actually." My voice definitely doesn't drop at the last bit. Or get wobbly. At all.

"Oh, too bad. I was going to ask if you'd want to join our book club next week. After all, you already know two of the members now."

"Do I?" Okay, my voice is definitely sad and shaky. Because of course, I want to join Rachel's book club. Of course, I want to move to Magnolia Cove and spend my days elbow-deep in bread dough and slowly write food stories while overlooking the wild stretch of beach—and maybe fall in love with a certain baker.

"Hey, Zoe," Rachel calls out.

Zoe emerges from the back with her signature grin in place. "Tired of eating ice cream all the time and wanted to try some real desserts?" Then to me, "Her husband owns the fancy ice cream place in town. You should try it out before you leave, City Girl."

"Hey!" Rachel props her hands on her hips. "Grant makes all his ice cream recipes from scratch. He just launched a new flavor this week."

"Salted caramel brownie." Zoe nudges me and whispers loudly enough for everyone to hear, "He stole the idea from Ethan."

"Who stole what from me?" Ethan asks as he walks up beside us, swiping his hands on a towel. My body warms at the nearness of his presence, the hum of his voice. It's like there's some magic in him, and every time we're together, it curls into my bones.

"Ethan, inform your co-worker that Grant did not steal his new flavor from you," Rachel says.

Ethan shrugs. "Hey, as long as he buys the brownies from me, I'm fine with him claiming the credit."

Zoe slugs Ethan in the arm. "He's too nice. That's basically him admitting it was his idea."

"Pfft." Rachel points at cookies in the display case, and Zoe bags them up for her. "See you at book club next week?"

"Nope. I told you, it's sci-fi or bust for me."

"Oh, come on, Zoe!"

"You guys have known each other for a while?" I ask.

"Basically forever." Rachel accepts the cookies and pops the bag into her woven tote.

"Band geeks for life." Zoe throws up her hand, and Rachel high-fives it. They both giggle.

I take Rachel's payment, but I've never felt more alone. Their uninhibited laughter, the shared history in their eyes— it's like a free sample of an ingredient I can't afford. I have Tish, but I'm always working, always traveling, always too busy chasing the next byline to build the kind of life that comes with book clubs, inside jokes, and showing up just because.

When Rachel leaves, Zoe flips the sign to close, wishes me goodbye, and best of luck writing up my five-star review of the Whisk. She gives another giant grin, then locks the door on her way out. I should say goodbye to Ethan and follow her out, but I can't. My feet feel cemented to the tile. There's nothing left to clean, yet I'm unable to move. Ethan moves past me to wrap up the few remaining baked goods out of the case, then he takes a deep breath and stands. "Stay longer?"

Heat floods my cheeks, and I'm still at a loss for words, still stuck. Even without understanding what he's asking, a part of me wants to say yes.

Ethan turns back to the pastries and begins shoving them into the box like he doesn't care if he breaks the entire batch. "Jas—the kid I mentor—is coming by in a few minutes to bake something. Would you like to join us?"

I should say no.

I should say I have ten thousand unwritten words due (not a lie), and that I need to pack and maybe get one good night's sleep before traveling home. But with Ethan Hart looking at me like that—like I'm the only thing in this room worth noticing, like maybe he regrets Zoe interrupting us earlier this week and wishes he'd kissed me anyway—I can't.

"I'd love to."

Ethan's smile is sunshine. He turns back to his task and neatly packs away the remaining baked goods that I've learned he'll drop by the local soup kitchen on his way home.

A boy—maybe nine years old—with a shock of auburn hair and bright green eyes knocks on the door. Ethan walks over and lets him in. The kid ditches his backpack into a booth. It falls, hitting the floor with a thud, but he seems not to notice. "Ethan! I need help!"

Ethan kneels beside him and puts a hand on his shoulder. If I could capture an image of him for the magazine—that would be the one. His entire attention given to this child, his eyes relaxed and soft blue, his apron soiled from the day's work. It's too intimate of an interaction, though, so I don't go for my camera.

"Hey, buddy, breathe and tell me what's going on."

Jas rubs the palms of his hands into his eyes. "It's so stupid. It's just that I really messed up. I bragged to the guys at school that I have the world's best cupcake recipe, and they signed me up to bring some for show and tell tomorrow."

Ethan tilts his head to the side, his expression going soft, his lips lifting at the corners. "You make excellent cupcakes, Jas."

"There's a difference between excellent and world's best."

"Of course I'll help you. But have you met Ms. Sinclair yet?"

Ethan gestures to me, and Jas flips around. Color drains from his face until only the freckles over his nose keep a hint of warmth. "Oh, Ms. Sinclair. Umm, actually I just remembered

I promised my mom to, umm, take out the trash this after-noon. See you later, Ethan!"

Ethan lifts his hand like he might stop the boy, but Jas snatches his backpack and flies out the door.

There's a beat of quiet as Ethan slowly rises to his feet. I pull my apron off. "I must have forgotten that I had my snake hair on today."

Ethan chuckles, but it's forced and echoes around the space. "Jas is... a bit skittish, that's all."

The way he says the words, I know it's part of the lies he continues weaving. I don't understand what about, though. And the fear in Jas's wide eyes? The journalist in me wants to extend my stay. I've yet to discover whatever's bubbling just below Magnolia Cove's beautiful exterior.

But I can't linger. I've already extended my trip, and it's time to return to my life—to train whistles blaring at night, stacks of bills piled on countertops, and putting down my writer's pencil for an editor's pen.

My return tickets—one for the ferry and one for the plane ride—sit on my dresser at the B&B like bad omens. The weight of these thoughts feels like boulders pressing on my shoulder blades. Outside, the sky has gone dark, clouds rolling across the sunset.

Ethan pulls his apron off too and tosses it into the laundry basket. "Can I walk you back to the B&B?"

"That would be great."

We exit, and I try to soak it all in—the teal awning I'd found trite not so long ago, the gleaming glass Zoe wages war with a microfiber towel every day to achieve, the cobblestone streets that seem to lead here, directly to the Whisk.

I've still not started my exposé. I can't bring myself to tear this place down. It feels like home. Like if I write something that destroys it, that would be the same as ripping apart mine and Missy's childhood memories. But thinking of my sister reminds me she needs this raise and the security it would bring. I just have to make it through one more semester—and find a miracle that pays off all my bills—then I can follow my dreams. I won't achieve any of that if I stay in Magnolia Cove. *Gastronomy Eats* probably wouldn't keep me on as staff. My mouth dries at the thought.

I'm one of those rare, lucky people who gets paid well for doing something she loves. A few weeks in a Christmas-special town and working alongside the world's best-looking baker, who apparently actually has a heart of gold, has me ready to throw it all away. Alex from a month ago would be appalled at my thoughts. She'd remind me of the years of hard work, the writing for pennies while in college to gain experience, and turning in twice as many articles as anyone else as an intern. The late nights, takeaway meals, and sacrifices stacked up like stepping stones.

But the Alex I am now, walking the quiet streets of Magnolia Cove beside Ethan, isn't so sure. This place, these people—they've awakened something within me. A longing for a life filled with more than bylines and deadlines. For a life that might have a story I can actually sink into for once.

Ethan seems equally lost in thought, his face lifted to the sky as if he's searching for answers in the cloud-covered stars. I wonder what secrets and hopes he hides behind those deep, blue eyes. I wonder if I'll ever be satisfied not knowing the answer.

One minute, I'm studying Ethan, his sharp jawline and thick lips, and the next, I'm gasping. Rain heaves from the sky as though someone turned a bucket over. There's no gentle sprinkle as a warning. It's cool and cloudy one minute, pouring the next.

Ethan lets out a laugh, the sound rich even over the patter of rain. It breaks away my bad feelings, sending them rushing toward the gutters with the storm.

"Come on," he says, grabbing my hand. "Run!"

Laughing, we dash for it, our feet splashing through quickly forming puddles. Cool rain splatters my skin and soaks through my clothes in seconds. But Ethan's hand is warm in mine, and I find I don't mind the impromptu shower.

By the time we reach the shelter of the B&B's porch, we're both soaked to the skin. Ethan's t-shirt is plastered against his muscular chest in a way that leaves no room for imagination. Waves crash in the distance, louder now, and salt hangs in the air, mingling with the fresh, earthy scent of rain. Magnolia Cove is quiet, shrouded in the storm's peacefulness.

Ethan looks down at me, raindrops clinging to his eyelashes. His lips part, but he doesn't speak. My heart thunders. He's beautiful. Not just handsome, but beautiful in a way that makes my chest ache.

Before I can overthink it, I close the distance between us.

I tilt my face up so our breaths mingle and grip his rain-damp arm. Ethan tenses, his eyes widen, and he seems like he might pull away. A decision flickers across his expression, then he exhales softly, leans down, and closes the remaining space between us.

For a moment, there's no rainstorm, no beach, no bed & breakfast, or return tickets. There's only the warmth of Ethan's mouth, the gentle pressure of his hand on my waist, the rhythmic slide of his thumb over my hip bone. I can taste the rain on his lips, feel the heat of his skin through his damp shirt.

When we break apart, I'm dizzy, breathless. Ethan's not looking at me but out toward the sky again, his brow furrowed. My heart quits its ridiculous dancing and sinks as an icy feeling of doubt creeps in. Paired with my soaked clothing, it leaves me shivering. Maybe Ethan regrets the kiss. Maybe I've read the energy between us completely wrong.

"I know you're about to leave," he says, his voice husky, "but before you do, I'd love to show you a part of the town you haven't seen yet."

His gaze flicks back to me, and he shoves his hands into his pockets. There's a nervous energy radiating from him, about what, I'm not sure.

Once again, I should say no. We're two different people from two different worlds. As much as I want to daydream, my real life is in a city over five hundred miles from here. I should go inside, pack my bags, and leave this town and its secrets behind. But looking at Ethan, at the hope in his eyes, at the way the porch light gleams in the raindrops that dust his curls, I find I can't. Screw it. Just this once, I'm letting myself want. Letting myself have something I want for once.

"Yes," I whisper. "I'd love to."

Ethan's lips—the firm but soft ones that were just pressed against mine—break into a grin. His voice, though, is still gravelly, like he's struggling to speak. "There's the monthly farmer's market tomorrow. the Whisk closes and runs a booth. It's Zoe's turn to manage it, which means she'll spend half the day flirting with Mia and the other half handing out 'free samples' that are full-sized." His smile turns fond. "I'd love to show you around if you're interested."

I know I shouldn't. I have a deadline, an article to write, a life to get back to in New York. Standing here, rain-soaked and happier than I've been in years, I realize I don't want to go back. Not yet. Maybe not ever.

"I'd love to," I say before I can let logic win out. The dimples that appear in Ethan's cheeks when he smiles make it all feel worth it.

He leans in and presses a soft kiss to my cheek. "Goodnight, Alex."

"Goodnight, Ethan," I whisper.

As I watch him walk away, his tall form disappearing into

the mist, I realize I'm in trouble. I came here to write a simple article, uncover a few secrets, and move on with my life.

Instead, I'm discovering things I didn't know I was looking for. A place that feels like forever with its quaint streets and friendly faces. People who feel like the family Missy and I don't have. And Ethan. A man who makes me believe in magic.

I huff a breath and go inside, prepared to fight with the internet to reroute my travel plans again.

Ethan

Asking Alex to stay was a mistake. I shove my hands into my pockets as people spill past me. The Magnolia Cove Farmer's Market is always a riot of color and smells, like the best parts of a county fair distilled into a few picturesque streets. One of the great things about a small town is how everyone comes together for everything. This is, by far, not our most interesting event, yet I invited Alex here as a desperate plea for her to stay.

But right now, I'm just waiting. Waiting for her.

"Stay longer," I'd whispered to her in the bakery's afternoon dim. I'd meant to ask her to stay and help with Jas, but maybe I also meant more. Which is stupid, because if she knew the truth about me—if the council would even let her find out my truth—she'd run from here and never look back.

Mrs. Delehay walks up, her Pomeranian on a leash tiptoeing beside her. I always forget the creature can actually walk on its own during the rare times she lets it down. She winks and pats my shoulder. "I have the perfect dessert idea picked out for Bridge club this week, dear."

"Read it in one of your magazines?" I'm pretty certain we subscribe to several of the same ones now.

She raises her nose just a tad higher in the air and smirks in a way that makes it hard for me not to smile. "Nope, got some advice from the city girl."

"Alexandra?"

"Mhmm. I'll place my order on Monday."

"You know, Mrs. Delehay, if you already know what you want, you could tell me now."

She lifts the pup into her arms. "Pah. Now where would be the fun in that?"

Without another word, she wanders off toward the vendors, and I release a sigh. If Zoe were here, she'd laugh until tears formed in her eyes. Zoe loves when someone flusters me. She thinks it's humorous to play with fate.

I don't know what Alex suggested for Mrs. Delehay. It could end up actually being something outside my skill set or something I lack the ingredients to produce. But I somehow doubt Alex would set me up to fail.

All week, she's shared stories about her life, misadventures in her world travels, late nights with a stiff back as she typed away to meet a deadline, and—most affectionately—reminiscences of time spent with her sister. I've offered her bits and pieces of myself along the way, as much as I can, at least. I want to give her everything: tell her why I'm stuck here in the Cove, why maybe it's growing on me, and why Jas feared her. Because the council isn't happy she's stayed this long, and every magical resident has been warned to keep their secrets buried deep. Parents of kids like Jas have told them to steer clear, afraid that one slip—one moment of unguarded magic —could unravel everything.

I'd stopped by his house the night before to check on him after I'd dropped Alex off at the B&B. After we'd shared that kiss that felt like tasting Porcelana chocolate for the first time. Complex and simple, pure yet filled with fire.

The taste of Alex was still on my lips when I sat with Jas on his house's front stoop.

"Ethan, everyone says she's going to find out about our magic. Mom says she's dangerous!"

He'd released a slow breath through his nose, and I tried to think with my brain instead of my heart for once. *I'll keep you safe, buddy, I promise.*

Jas had looked up, and his furrowed brow and tense shoulders melted away. Like he had perfect faith in me. It had been a long time since anyone had offered me so much. I couldn't throw it away.

And that's why inviting Alex to stay for another day was a mistake. Especially when Dean Markham had made it clear she needed to leave as quickly as possible. The goal was to let the Whisk make a good impression and then send her on her way. Instead, I found myself sneaking around the bakery all week, using Zoe or some of our employees as distractions, so I could infuse magic into the food without Alex noticing. Instead, I found myself kissing her in the rain and wishing she'd stay forever. That kind of idiocy is exactly what cost me my freedom.

I've just about talked myself into leaving the farmer's market and standing Alex up when she walks through the entrance. She's wearing a pair of fitted jeans that hug her hips and a simple t-shirt, yet something about the material makes it drape perfectly around her curves. Her hair is pulled back into a curled ponytail, and her eyes search the crowd. When they land on me, they light up. My heart warms, and before I can continue my litany of protestations, I walk to meet her.

"Alex." I'm not sure what the protocol is for greeting her. The last time I saw her, I walked away with her chapstick's vanilla flavor on my lips.

"Morning, Chief." If she's feeling any nerves, she's not showing them. She tucks her hands into her pockets as she looks around. "So, this is the must-see farmer's market?"

I shrug and start walking. It's difficult to look at her eyes glowing golden in the sunlight and not want to kiss her again. To hear that nickname she's dubbed me with—one that apparently means she finds me attractive and competent—and not want more. But I can't have more with her, for a million reasons.

One of them sits at a picnic table, his black leather jacket on even in the heat. He narrows his eyes in my direction. I give Dean a head bob and move on. Alex frowns in his direction but keeps to my side. There will be hell to pay later, but I'll face it to capture even a few more hours with Alex.

We pass a gazebo where Rachel leads her band students in a lively song. Grant has set his ice cream cart next to it, and I offer him a wave. Alex does the same to Rachel, who grins and returns the gesture before turning in time to catch a twelve-year-old's flute that he nearly drops. Alex's laugh feels like opening a fresh batch of cinnamon, rich and full of possibilities. She already recognizes people here, and my heart wants to dream, wants to believe that Alex might love it here. That she might want to move here. Might want someone here.

But that's ridiculous. Alex isn't even magical.

We pass Mia and Zoe. The latter shoots finger guns at us, which makes Alex smile until her cheeks fill with color. A slip of golden hair spills free from her hair tie and curves against her cheek. I'm desperate to touch it.

"Oh, look." Alex walks toward another booth. It's Jas's mother's soap stand, filled with bars and bottles. As we move closer, the air fills with the scents of lavender and honey, mint and coconut. On the table's end, Jas has set up a homemade sign: *Jas's Sweetcakes!*

A few dozen cupcakes are stacked around the sign, and

when we reach him, a grin spreads across my face. When Jas first started spending time with me, he fumbled over his words and would shrug if someone asked him if he enjoyed baking.

"Do we have our newest market vendor?" I ask.

Jas flips his attention to me and then bounces on his toes. "Ethan! I was wondering if you'd come today." His gaze drifts to Alex, and he smiles. He's so much more at ease today. He truly believes I'm going to keep him safe. And I must.

"We sure do," says his mother, Olivia, who has her red hair braided back and tucked beneath a sunhat. She offers me a wink. "All thanks to you, Ethan."

"Nah. You can't beat natural talent, which Jas has in spades. All I did was offer a little help. What do you have for sale, Jas?"

His cheeks flare with a bit of color, but he doesn't break my gaze. It makes me damn proud of the kid and how far he's come. "Well, last night I thought: What might Ethan suggest we make? So, I decided to try a brand-new cupcake recipe on my own. I'm calling them Courage Cupcakes!"

"Did you really?" I ask. "What flavor?"

He waggles his eyebrows. "Surprise flavor."

Alex chuckles and pulls a ten-dollar bill free. "I'd love to purchase one. We could all use some courage now and then."

Jas accepts the money, tries to make change, which Alex refuses, and then picks the cake with the cleanest frosting. A dusting of gold stars glisten over the surface.

Olivia looks at me from beneath her hat, and my ears burn with the gratitude in her expression. I haven't really done much. Not enough to deserve this look, this quiet acknowledgment.

But something about Magnolia Cove is making me realize what it means to feel roots for the first time in my life. To want to sink down into the soil and let them spread. To belong. I've spent so long thinking of this place as a cage, but maybe—just maybe—it's something else entirely.

Then Alexandra walks into my life, reminding me of why I never have before.

"See you later, Jas." Alex and I both wave goodbye. He waves back and then turns to another approaching customer.

Alex splits the cupcake, and I accept my half and take a bite. Citrusy orange flavor bursts across my tongue right about the time the honey cream cheese frosting hits, balancing the flavor. An extra spark of energy sizzles through the treat—there's a bit of magic infused in them too.

If it's for courage, I might be in trouble. I'm already acting stupidly around Alex without it.

"It's good," Alex says. She takes another nibble, then rolls the bite around in her mouth. When she swallows, I shiver.

"The kid's good."

"Sounds like he has an excellent mentor."

I snort. All Jas needed was a little encouragement. He's a natural and would have excelled with or without me.

A handful of people hustle by, canvas bags filled with vegetables and flowers. Alex finishes the last bite of the Courage Cupcake. "When I read that article about you in *Food Frenzy*, I thought you were fake."

"That's funny, because when I read the first article written by you, I thought it was the realest thing I'd ever experienced."

Her lips part, and her eyes widen, but before she can respond, we approach the booth I've been looking for. "Dad," I call out. "Meet Ms. Alexandra Sinclair."

Dad jumps up from behind his vegetable stand, patting his assistant's shoulder before walking around to us. He's wearing flannel and jeans paired with a wide-brimmed hat. It took Robert Hart exactly fifteen minutes to adjust to the Magnolia Cove lifestyle, and he's loved it every second since.

"Please, call me Robert." He thrusts out a work-worn

hand to Alex, who accepts it warmly. "Any friend of Ethan's is a friend of mine. Though"—he squints at me—"he failed to mention how beautiful you are."

I groan. "Dad," I drag the word out, but I'm smiling. For one thing, his comment has brought another round of color flushing Alex's cheeks, and damn, is she beautiful when that happens.

Dad lifts one silver-streaked eyebrow. "You know, if you need information for your magazine article, I'm the person to speak with."

"Is that right?" Alex asks.

"Mhmm. Ethan wasn't always the baking prodigy he is today."

Okay, this was officially a mistake. "I brought her to say hello as requested. The least you could do is try to behave yourself."

Alex's breath catches, and she tilts her face in my direction. I find that I can't meet her gaze and instead focus on the dozens of different tomatoes stacked across the stand—some violet and the size of softballs, others petite and fire-red. Does she think me introducing her to my dad means more? Would she want that? I shouldn't want that, so I don't know why I'm entertaining the thought.

Dad leans against the stand's corner and crosses his ankles. "Has he told you about the Great Birthday Cake Disaster of '98?"

Heat rushes up my neck. This is my opportunity to have my baking featured in a world-renowned magazine, and it's going to end up with ridiculous anecdotes because I foolishly agreed to let my father meet Alex.

"Dad, no—"

"I'm certainly curious," Alex says. She peers up at me from beneath her long lashes, her eyes sparkling, and I can't help but smile back. "Go on, Mr. Hart."

"Call me Robert." He winks. "Anyway, this ambitious little baker"—he shoves an elbow my way—"decides he's going to make his mother a rainbow birthday cake."

I cover my face with my hands. "Can we not?"

"Shush you." Dad swats my arm gently, then waves at friends who pass by before continuing. "Well, turns out our little artist here decided to mix his colors directly on the kitchen counter. By the time I got there, that white Formica was a Jackson Pollock painting of food coloring. No amount of scrubbing could get it out."

I drag a hand back through my hair. "We had a tie-dye kitchen counter for years after that."

"Sure did. Your mother called it her 'abstract art installation.' Said it brightened up the entire kitchen. We only replaced it when we remodeled, and I swear she was sad to see it go."

"Yeah, I think I was too."

Alex is looking at both of us with a divot pressed between her brows. I have the urge to reach for her hand, but that's the last thing I need to do in front of Dad. I'd never hear the end of it. He still thinks Sarah was too immature for me, as if I wasn't the problem in that situation. He still thinks I have a right to meet someone and fall in love. He's wrong, but it's nice to know he's always stood in my corner, no matter how badly I've screwed things up.

"It sounds like you two make quite the team," Alex says.

Dad throws his arm around me. "Always have, always will. Even when this one insisted on living on an island in the middle of nowhere, I said, 'Ethan, you can't get rid of me that easily.'"

My muscles tense. Dad's just teasing, and Alex probably thinks nothing of it. But he's dancing precariously close to truths she can't know about.

"Dad," I say, hoping the word doesn't sound too terse.

He throws his hand in surrender. "I know, I know." He gives me a wink, and I fight a sigh of exasperation before he runs off, telling one story after another. About my first attempt at sourdough ("I swear, that starter was alive and plotting world domination") and about the time I entered a pie-eating competition at the county fair ("He won, but I don't think he could look at a cherry for months.")

All throughout, Alex laughs, asks questions, and keeps shooting me small, meaningful glances that leave me wishing I could read her mind. And wishing for things that can't happen.

"All right," Dad finally calls. "I've held you two up for long enough. Grammie Rae expects you to stop for some honey candy, though."

Alex and Dad say goodbye, then he lifts his eyebrows at me. I can already hear the words he'd say if she wasn't around: Smart and pretty? You've done worse, son. I roll my eyes but clap him on the shoulder before leading Alex through the crowd of residents and tourists.

"Honey candy?" Alex asks.

"It's a Magnolia Cove specialty if you want to try it."

Grammie Rae has shoved her curly silver hair beneath a ball cap, and she stirs her massive copper pot. When we walk up, she claps her hands. "I'd hoped you'd stop by."

"So, I hear. We'll take two, Grammie Rae, and this is Alexandra Sinclair."

"Nice to meet you. Everyone around here calls me Grammie." She scoops the warm honey taffy out of the pot and into a cone, handing one to Alex. "You can call me that too."

Before she releases the treat, her fingers light with energy. A spark of magic glistens along the golden, sticky candy. Alex gasps and nearly drops the cone. I've stopped breathing altogether. Revealing our magic to non-magic wielders is the number one rule we must never break. It's the rule I broke that got me placed on parole here. If Dean Markham was around... But Grammie Rae shoots me a wink, like she isn't worried in the least about Dean Markham, and hands me my paper cone. I pay her and thank her, but the words come out choked.

Alex continues to stare at the candy, and my voice is gruff when I speak. "It's best warm."

She's staring at the cone like it's about to come alive. She saw something. A journalist from New York City just saw something. I should report it. I should find Dean right this minute. Alex lifts the paper cup and takes the first bite of the honey candy. Her eyes go wide.

Even without tasting mine yet, I know the flavor she's experiencing. The impossibly smooth, warm honey and the burst of sweetness. I've experimented but never came close to whatever Grammie Rae does to achieve the consistency.

"Oh my god," she moans, and it sends a shiver down my spine. "This is incredible."

I grin. Maybe she didn't notice the magic. Maybe it's fine. She lifts her face, her eyes amber in the sunlight, matching the candy shimmering in her paper cone and another glistening spot by her lip.

"Oh, wait, you've got a bit..." I reach out with my thumb and swipe the candy away. The minute my finger scrapes her flesh, a jolt rushes through me, and we both freeze.

"There," I whisper and force myself to pull my hand away. "All clean."

Alex doesn't acknowledge my words. I'm not even sure she's breathing. Her expression reminds me of how she looked on the porch—rain-drenched, her hair darkened, her eyes wide and unblinking. I'm going to kiss her in front of everyone, and I don't even care.

"Alex!" Rachel walks up, Mia at her side.

Alex jumps, then turns and walks toward them, immediately starting a conversation. I should go with her, but I turn back to Grammie Rae. "You used magic," I whisper.

She stirs the pot, and her dark eyes twinkle. "Mhmm, been known to do that now and then."

"Yes, but in front of Ms. Sinclair?"

"Oh, it's Ms. Sinclair now, is it? With the way you two were just looking at each other, I was starting to think Mrs. Hart."

"Grammie Rae, I know you mean well—"

She stops my speech with a dramatic sweep of her arm, and her voice gets low and serious. "She saw it. The magic." My furrowed brow must give away my confusion, but Grammie Rae sets her stirring spoon down and walks closer to me, her voice low and serious. "Most of the tourists can't see a thing. The wards, you know? But you saw that Ms. Sinclair did."

She had. I'd heard the gasp slip from her mouth and watched her lips part. It's true. Even though we're not supposed to use magic in front of others out of an abundance of caution, most people can't see it. But Alex had.

"Magic chooses people it wants sometimes," Grammie Rae says.

"What do you mean?"

She nods over to where Alex is embroiled in a laughter-filled conversation with Mia and Rachel, like they'd all graduated school together and not like they'd just met.

"I'm saying the magic is choosing Alex. She belongs here with us. Hmm?"

I'm about to ask more questions, demand a better answer, but then Alex walks back over, and Grammie Rae gets that twinkle in her eye again. "Tell me now, Ms. Sinclair"—at this, she grins at me—"has Ethan here informed you about the Bonanza?"

Alex turns to me, her brow furrowed, a smile still lingering from her conversation with her new friends. Panic ripples through me, a stone dropped into a lake. Dean Markham wanted Alex gone two weeks ago. He would not approve of extending her stay yet again.

"Grammie, Ms. Sinclair has important deadlines and—"

"Nonsense!" Grammie lifts the spoon and waves it, sticky bits of honey candy dripping down the handle. "This is the food-lover's event of the season. Ever since he's moved here, Ethan has won every year. Frankly, it's time someone gave him some actual competition." Her lips curl into a grin. "What do you say, Ms. Sinclair? Care to show our local baker extraordinaire how it's done in the city?"

I clear my throat. "I wouldn't say I win every year." It's a weak deflection, and I'm not motivated to argue, anyway. I should be. I should encourage Alex to return home. Discourage whatever this is building between us. But I'm not the one asking her to stay this time, and what could a few more days hurt, anyway?

"Oh, hush," Grammie Rae says. "False modesty doesn't suit you, dear. You're cute enough without it." She turns toward Alex. A handful of curious customers have wandered up to the booth, but Grammie's entire attention remains fixed on us. "Please say you'll stay. It would mean so much to have a food expert give our local celebrity baker some competition."

The hair that's come free of Alex's ponytail sticks to the part of her cheek that I'd brushed the candy away from. She's holding her cone so tightly she dents the paper. "I... I suppose I could try to rearrange some things."

A breath rushes out of me. I was sure she'd say no. I still can't believe that she seems to want to be here. To be with me. Her gaze meets mine at that moment, and my heart thunders.

"Wonderful!" Grammie Rae claps. "Oh, everyone will be so excited. A real New York City food writer in our little contest. I'm going to spread the word." She bustles forward, greeting the next customer.

Alex peeks up beneath the wisps of her windswept hair, and my heart stops pounding for a moment. Grammie Rae's words echo through my mind. Magic chooses people it wants.

Hope is the world's most painful emotion. Even allowing myself to imagine that Alex might be different, that she might love the Cove, love—other things in the Cove. I shiver.

"What did I just agree to?" she asks.

I chuckle. "Let's just say you might want to bring a change of clothes." I look down at her leather flats. "And maybe leave any shoes you care about at the B&B."

Alex

"What do you think is appropriate clothing to milk a cow in?"

I'm digging through the limited wardrobe I've packed for Magnolia Cove. Despite not knowing the answer, I'm pretty sure silk and cashmere are definitely not it. I shift the phone and wedge it between my ear and shoulder.

"Wait," Tish says, her voice muffled over the phone line, "do you plan to milk a cow?"

"It's apparently part of the competition. Everyone has to gather their ingredients fresh around the farm while under a time limit."

There's a beat of silence, filled only with static over the line, before Tish bursts into laughter, the sound blending with the clatter of her tea plates. "Girl, you've got it bad."

I stand in front of the mirror, holding up the only pair of jeans I've packed. I never once imagined wearing them on an actual farm. Some food writers scale mountains and trek into the wild to discover where their ingredients come from. I've always been more comfortable in Michelin-starred dining rooms.

I look at myself in the mirror—really look. My skin's

picked up some color from Magnolia Cove's sunshine, I've embraced the beachy waves, and there's something in my posture—like I've finally let go, finally relaxed.

"Oh god," I whisper, "what if I do?"

Tish squeals through the phone. "Don't say that like it's a bad thing. When was the last time you felt this way about someone, honey?"

I sink onto the bed, still clutching the jeans, a million thoughts tumbling through my head. "I... I don't know. This is crazy. I'm here to write an article, not fall for some small-town baker with impossibly blue eyes."

"Girl, you're doing us all a favor. Do you know how many people are in love with him on ClipClop?"

"No one," I say, defensively. Then, softer, "I just mean, no one really knows the real him. He's not just gorgeous, he's kind. And patient. You should see him with Jas, this kid he mentors. It's like... he sees the best in everyone, and helps bring it out. And Ethan as a baker? He's amazing. He really gets it."

There's a pause, but not because the line cut out. In the background, I hear the usual hum of Celestial Sips' morning crowd.

"Oh god, I do have it bad, don't I?" I groan, my voice full of disbelief. "What am I doing? This isn't me. I don't fall for guys I write about. I don't take part in farm baking contests. I don't..."

"Live a little?" Tish finishes, her voice gentle. "Alex, honey, when was the last time you did something because it made you happy? Not for work, not for your sister—just for you?"

I flop back onto the bed, the quilt and embroidered pillows catching me. "I... I don't know."

"Exactly," Tish says, soft but firm. "Maybe this ridiculous farm baking contest is exactly what you need. And maybe

Ethan-the-baking-hunk is, too. You don't have to marry him, you know. Just... enjoy the moment."

I sit up, catching my reflection in the mirror again. The woman looking back at me seems different—lighter, more open. "Maybe you're right. But that doesn't solve my immediate problem. What am I going to wear to milk a cow in?"

Tish bursts into laughter on the other end of the line. "It's too much to ask for video evidence of this event, isn't it?"

I scowl, but she laughs even harder, and despite my annoyance, I can't help but smile. "Here's what you're going to do. Find the local general store. Buy yourself some sturdy boots, a pair of overalls, and the most ridiculous flannel shirt you can find."

"Overalls?" Okay, calling Vivian to ask for yet another extension—and hearing her opinion of me sink with every word—might no longer be the most horrifying part of this decision.

Tish is cracking up, though. At least one of us is having a good day. "The morning rush is picking up. I've got to go. If you love me, you'll send me pictures later."

As I hang up, a smile tugs at my lips. Maybe Tish is right. About everything except the flannel. There are lines I won't cross.

I look back at the mirror, the woman reflected in it holding my gaze with a certainty I'm not sure I've ever seen before. I can't explain it, but Magnolia Cove feels like home, even though I've only been here a few weeks. There's something different here. Something... magical.

I release a breath and straighten up. Regardless of how enchanting this trip feels, I still have to write the article about the Whisk. Vivian won't accept the sugary, charming spin I'm tempted to take. It's just a little too cotton-candy sweet for *Gastronomy Eats*. Maybe that's been the problem all along. Maybe I'm tired of gnawing at bitter roots because they're 'avant-garde.' Maybe I want something that actually feeds the soul. Something warm, indulgent, and undeniably real.

I think of Ethan's rough finger scraping honey candy from my cheek, the way his eyes had darkened.

There's nothing fake or manufactured about the Whisk or its owner. Nothing to critique about how Ethan kneads every loaf of bread by hand, or orders random, expensive ingredients to experiment with, always exploring. And there's no flaw in how Zoe knows exactly when to surprise a regular with a box of treats 'just because.'

But 'small-town bakery'? That's not palatable enough for the Manhattan brunch crowd to scroll through between sips of mimosa. It's too kitschy. Not pretentious enough. It lacks that sense of intrigue for people who can eat their way around the world in a single block.

My journal lays open on the side table. The first line I've written for the article glares at me. *The Whimsical Whisk relies heavily on small-town charm to mask its...*

It's what Vivian wants me to write, but I haven't even been able to finish the first sentence. Whatever I write after this will be a lie. But this is who I am. This is what I've worked so hard to become.

Isn't it?

I slam the journal shut and shove it into the table's drawer. I'll think about that later. For now, I need to purchase a pair of overalls.

* * *

That's how I find myself dressed in a pair of overalls and a t-shirt that says Magnolia Cove: Small Town, Big Wonders, along with a pair of surprisingly comfortable emerald boots when Ethan drives up to the B&B.

He's behind the wheel of an old blue pickup truck—the

kind you see in butter commercials and holiday rom-coms. The truck rumbles when he cuts the ignition. As Ethan jumps out, my breath catches.

He's wearing a simple white t-shirt that clings to his muscular arms and chest, along with a pair of well-worn jeans. He drags his fingers back through his hair, and if I hadn't gotten to know how humble and self-effacing he was, I'd think he was doing it just to show off those perfectly sculpted abs. People shouldn't be able to consume so much sugar and still look like that. It's a crime.

"Well, well," he says, his voice warm. "Look who's gone native."

I shove my hands into the overall pockets and pull them wide, stretching the material out. They're surprisingly comfortable. "When in Rome, right?" I shrug. "Or should I say, when in Magnolia Cove? Besides, someone suggested I should leave any clothing I appreciated at the inn."

His gaze runs up me slowly, assessing. It feels like he's touching me—fingers tracing along my thighs, over my arms, his breath warm against my neck. When he speaks, his voice goes gravelly. "It suits you."

The way he says the words, I think he means more than just the clothes. Like maybe Magnolia Cove itself fits me. Like I belong here. If only that could be true.

He walks around to the passenger door and opens it. "I'd hate to be late bringing the celebrity to the big Bonanza."

I laugh, but it's mostly out of relief that he broke the tension. When I walk up to the truck, he offers his hand, and I accept. His fingers gripping mine cause me to shiver, and I don't jump into the truck. Instead, I turn toward Ethan, and he's already leaning down towards me, his mouth impossibly close to mine.

I keep thinking about that kiss—how it felt like a whispered secret, how I wish I could ask more questions with the rest of my body until I understood it.

"We'll be late," Ethan whispers, his breath brushing my cheek.

"Right. Of course." I hop into the truck. He shudders, then shuts the door, like that was a struggle for him too. I take a deep breath and try to center myself. The truck is rich with scents—cloves, leather, and grass. Ethan jumps into the driver's seat and cranks the engine with another rumbling purr that vibrates through the bench seat.

"I wouldn't have guessed you drove a truck."

He grins, and my heart is doing stupid somersaults. Tish was right. I'm head-over-heels, doodle-his-name-in-the-margins, melt-like-a-puddle crushing on this man. It should be embarrassing. Instead, I slide closer and find the middle seat belt.

"I don't," Ethan says. "This truck is my dad's. The road out to the farm is pretty rough."

I click the seatbelt into place. Ethan seems to consider where I've chosen to sit, then slides his arm behind the seatrest. My stomach swoops as his skin grazes the back of my neck. "So, what do you drive, then... a vintage Vespa?"

Ethan releases a rumbling laugh that matches the truck as he pulls out of the driveway. He seems so at ease with the windows cracked and a breeze playing with his curls. "I rode one in Paris once, actually. Vowed to never do that again. But no, I actually have a '67 Beetle. It was my grandfather's."

"Oh... that's... unexpectedly cool."

"Unexpectedly?" He looks out of the corner of his eyes at me, then fixes his gaze back on the road that's taking us out of town. "I think a firefighter magazine model could drive a vintage car, and it would be expectedly cool."

I roll my eyes. "Don't let that comment go to your head, Chief."

He laughs. "I'll have to come up with another way to impress you, then. Any suggestions?"

"Hmm... Maybe you could juggle some eggs today? I interviewed a sous chef who could do that."

"Juggle eggs?" He slows as we ease onto another road that's bumpier. Every jostle rattles through the truck. "Please tell me someone didn't actually do that during an interview?"

"Oh, he absolutely did. Dropped a few too."

Ethan cringes, the secondhand embarrassment adorable on him. "Well, I'm glad I'm not the most incompetent person you've ever interviewed, at least."

The view changes as we drive on. Charming buildings give way to dark swathes of woods on one side and stretching, golden farmland on the other.

"You're not incompetent, Ethan. Far from it."

So far from that, it's making the job I came here to do very difficult. Thinking about betraying this man as I sit next to him in his dad's truck, fresh air whipping my ponytail back, his warmth sinking into my side, makes me want to ask him to pull over and let me out. Let me walk back into town with my head hanging in shame. His cheeks flush, which only makes me feel worse. I wish I could tell him he's too good for *Gastronomy Eats*—that we're becoming a watered-down imitation of authenticity—all dramatic photos and hollow buzzwords.

Ethan shrugs. "Maybe I can't juggle eggs, but I can gather them for today's event, at least."

"Gather them?" I echo, suddenly remembering the Bonanza. I sink down against the worn leather seat. "Oh god, that's right. We're going to have to do actual farm stuff today, aren't we?"

Ethan cocks an eyebrow. "Never been on a farm before? Renowned food writer, Alexandra Sinclair? What about all the farm-to-table, know-your-sourcing, sustainable-root dining trends?"

"I respect those trends." My back straightens as I shoot up and inadvertently draw closer to Ethan and his vanilla-rich scent. "I'm all about supporting farmers. I just don't want to actually... do the... farm stuff."

"Farm stuff." Ethan snorts. "Today is going to be really interesting. Come on, though. You've had to have visited a farm at some point in your life?"

Now it's my turn to blush. "I went to school in Greenwich. We took field trips to places like the New York Philharmonic or the Metropolitan Museum of Art. Not exactly places with, you know, cows or cornfields."

Ethan blows out a breath. "What made you decide to do the Bonanza, then?" He grins that easy smile that wrinkles his eyes. "I don't believe Grammie Rae is that convincing, despite what she thinks."

I chuckle, but the real reason for staying—the reason I'm still here—sits right next to me, driving his dad's old pickup truck, wind tousling his curls. I can't say that, though. Ethan looks over at me again, and it's like he can hear my thoughts, like the truth of them fills the limited space between us. I'm almost certain I can hear his heart pounding. The sun hits him, and he gleams like a statue of a Greek god, all sharp muscles and youthful beauty.

"I actually don't know how to milk a cow," I blurt out, needing to say anything to break the moment. "I'm going to have to make something dairy-free because I'm hopeless."

"I'll show you how."

"I thought we were celebrity rivals?"

His smile widens until his dimples show, and god, I hope we're getting out of this truck soon. If I have to spend another minute this close to him, I'm going to say or do something stupid. Something that definitely doesn't align with Alexandra Sinclair, renowned food writer who needs a raise.

"What can I say?" Ethan's still grinning. "I'm a sucker for a damsel in dairy distress."

"Dairy distress," I mutter. "If this is some scheme to improve your coolness factor, I'm pretty sure it ranks right up there with egg juggling."

"Ouch." He hooks his thumb around the wheel and turns it in a smooth motion that leaves me wondering what else his fingers can do. The truck pulls into a driveway, over a hill, then toward a farm—red barn and all. "I think you'll find cow-milking skills to be significantly more useful."

"We'll see," I grumble.

Ethan only laughs, but his hand drifts down toward my shoulder, and I lean into his touch. If this is what milking cows gets me, then I guess I'll take it.

Ethan

Alex Sinclair has absolutely no idea how to milk a cow. She's crouched on a wooden stool, swallowed by the adorable overalls she's donned, frowning at the animal. The rules state I can't physically help her, but attempting to talk her through it is just making things worse.

"Gently but firmly," I whisper. My own pail of milk sloshes softly as I shift my stance.

"That's what I've been doing," she says before timidly reaching toward the cow again.

Outside the barn, others shout as they gather their supplies, and the crowd cheers. This might actually be the year I lose by running out of time helping Alex. She clunks her bucket against the hay-scattered floor in frustration. The cow startles and flicks her tail before shooting Alex a glare.

This is entirely worth losing the competition for.

"You know, you could actually just make a dairy-free dessert," I offer.

"Children milk cows. I can do it too." She peers up at Grammie Rae in the far corner, who is watching us to make sure we follow the rules. "Just explain it one more time."

I sigh, but there's no mistaking the determination in her eyes—the same relentless drive that probably landed her at the top of her field. It's not just stubbornness; it's the refusal to back down from a challenge. The same trait that made her a force in journalism is now being applied to, apparently, dairy farming.

"You need to squeeze a little harder. Then glide your hand up and down like you're—" I trail off, and my cheeks heat. God, my thoughts around Alex lately have veered off a cliff. I can't stand near her without wishing I could touch her.

Alex looks back at me, and her expression has transformed into one of twinkling eyes and smirking lips. "Like I'm doing what, Chief?"

I clear my throat, and she bursts into a laugh. But something about the conversation must have inspired her, as she turns toward the bucket, and a hiss of milk hitting the pail sounds.

"Yes!" She cries, startling the cow again. She sinks down then pats the creature's side. "Sorry, girl."

The barn soon fills with the sound of sloshing milk. As soon as she's filled her pail enough, she jumps up, and we run back out toward the outdoor kitchen area.

The makeshift workspace is a flurry of activity. Contestants rush around, grabbing ingredients and fighting for stovetop space. Zoe furiously whisks something in one corner, her hair atypically disheveled, purple flyaways sticking to her sweaty brow.

"What are you making?" I call to her as I pass by, the strawberries I've gathered rocking in their bucket.

She grins maniacally. "Lavender-infused goat cheese ice cream with candied beets. It's going to be brilliant or disgusting. Maybe both!"

I roar with laughter. I really do love the Bonanza. The chaotic energy of it, the cheers from people in the crowd, including Jas, who has made a poster that says, "GO ETHAN! BAKE THOSE CAKES!" in wobbly letters. The smell of fresh-chopped onions and ripe tomatoes, and the sizzle of pans on portable burners, fills the air.

Alex appears at my elbow, her arms full of cucumbers and dill. She nods towards Jas. "Your protégé seems excited."

"He's a good kid." I grab a mixer and start whipping cream. Alex slices her cucumbers into thin circles, her brow furrowed.

"Chilled soup?" I guess.

She nods but doesn't look up. "Cucumber and dill with crème fraîche. It's such a beautiful summer day—perfect for it."

"Sounds fancy," I tease as I find my chef's knife and begin chopping strawberries. "You know the judges here prefer food that's never very... fussy, right?"

Alex shoots me a glare, but there's a hint of a smile on her lips. "I'll have you know cold soup was originally a humble dish meant to hydrate laborers who worked in the heat all day."

"Okay, sure, and that's exactly who eats gazpacho nowadays." I grab a free bowl and begin sifting ingredients for a dough.

"Are you saying my food is pretentious, Chief?"

"If the designer shoe fits..." I trail off and grin.

She tosses a piece of cucumber at me, and I catch it effortlessly. Her eyes widen in surprise. Behind her, I catch a glimpse of Dean Markham at the judges' table, his gaze sharp and calculating. He didn't miss that. My reflexes—unnatural reflexes, no ordinary person should have on display for a human journalist.

She doesn't understand how I can move that fast, and she never will. But if Grammie Rae is even partially right, Alex might be able to see something more, something hidden beneath the surface. It's always a problem when tourists start sensing more than they should. That's an issue for Dean Markham to deal with.

Normally, I'd be the first to voice my suspicions, but with Alex? I don't want Dean anywhere near her.

I know all too well what happens when the council decides someone knows too much. Dean doesn't wipe memories unless it's absolutely necessary—it's a last resort, and they only do it when magic is truly at risk. But magic is unpredictable, and when memories are erased, other things can go with them—names, moments, feelings.

I can't let that happen to Alex. I can't let them decide she's seen too much and take something from her—something she can never get back.

She's still staring at me, waiting for an answer. I try to act casual as I pop the cucumber into my mouth. I chew, swallow, then offer a playful smile. "Mm, delicious. Maybe you have a chance after all."

She snorts but turns back to her dish, a smile tugging at her lips.

The next hour speeds by in a blur of mixing, baking, and chilling. Before I know it, it's time to face the judges. We all line up with our creations in front of the panel of five—locals who love free treats and the attention more than they care about actually judging food. The real motivation for the contestants is the chance to try each other's creations, but there's always one exception: Dean Markham. His presence on the panel has raised more than a few eyebrows. He never participates in these events. But today, here he is, methodically tasting every dish, his eyes flickering between Alex and me.

I can't shake the feeling that something more than just food is on the line today.

Zoe's ice cream gets some raised eyebrows and hesitant tastes, but a few judges seem pleasantly surprised. It's not for me, but I like the idea of where she was going with it. She was only mildly curious about the culinary world when we met, but her interest has bloomed in the last few years.

When Dean tries Alex's soup, his expression remains carefully neutral, though I catch the slight tightening around his eyes. He writes something on his scorecard with sharp, precise movements. The other judges give appreciative nods, but nothing more than that. Then they dig into my dessert. The judges eat everything on their plate, and I realize the verdict before they make their announcement.

"And the winner is... Ethan Hart with his Classic Strawberry Shortcake."

The crowd erupts in cheers. Jas shakes his poster so hard the words blur. I can't help the smile stretching across my face. This town has wound its way into me like ivy claiming an old brick wall. I peek over at Alex, wondering if she's disappointed, but she's shaking her head with a wry smile.

"Ugh," she groans dramatically, but the smile remains. "I guess I should have taken your advice."

I lean in close, breathing in her sweet perfume scent blended with earthy hay and rich dill. "If it's any consolation, in an actual competition, your soup definitely would have won. It was sophisticated but not fussy and had the perfect balance of flavors."

"Flatterer." She ducks her head, and her hair spills over her cheek. I long to tuck it back, to let my fingers brush her soft skin again. "I suppose I'll have to up my game next time."

"Next time?" I can't help the hope that creeps into my voice. It's impossible, yet I cling to it. Maybe she'd choose to stay. Maybe she'd see me for who I really am and accept me.

Just as quickly, a knot forms in my stomach. I've let myself hope before, only to be bitterly disappointed. This time won't be any different—it can't be. Even people with their own magical abilities are wary of mine. I learned that early on. The way teachers watched me too closely, the way other kids' parents whispered behind my back. One slip-up, one moment of losing control, and suddenly I wasn't just another kid with magic—I was a problem to be managed.

Alex is human. If she saw my world, my reality, she'd never want any part of it. Even if magic calls to her like Grammie Rae suggested, that doesn't mean I do.

Alex shrugs as she finishes tidying up her station. "Well, I can't leave Magnolia Cove forever without a win to my name, can I?"

Hope sparks in my chest, bright and sudden, like a candle catching fire. I clench my teeth and force myself to focus on the task at hand, because with Dean's sharp gaze burning into my back, I should know better. I've already made mistakes that cost the council before, and Dean never lets me forget it.

As the crowds begin to disperse, Alex and I gather up the extra supplies—bowls, spoons, measuring utensils. We both reach for the same whisk at the same time, our fingers brushing. For a brief moment, I don't pull away. I let the warmth linger between us, just long enough to make my heart beat a little faster, then gently withdraw. I can't encourage this. Whatever this is between Alex and me, it's only going to end in her getting hurt.

And that's a price I'm not willing to pay.

"Ready to head back to the inn?" I gesture towards Dad's pickup.

"Yes, I'm exhausted and desperately need a shower."

I want to tell her that's the last thing she needs. That I'd love to hold her close and smell the earth-fresh scent on her. Brush the hair away from her neck as my knuckles follow its curve. Peel her clothes back. I close my eyes and walk towards the truck. That's the last place my mind needs to go.

Alex follows, and we both climb in. Like before, she slides into the middle seat, wedged between me and the door, her shoulder brushing mine as she buckles in. The truck purrs as we drive down the winding country road. The sun sets beyond the tree line, painting the sky in dramatic splashes of tangerine and peach.

Alex stares out the window, the browns of her eyes reflecting the sunset's gold. She sighs, then looks up at me. "What if I don't want to return to the inn yet?"

My breath catches, and in that single inhale, I breathe her in: sweet floral notes still lingering above the farm-fresh earthiness. She's settled beside me, her body warm, her head resting on my arm. "What would you rather do?"

I don't add: you could talk me into anything. You could talk me into bad decisions and regrets. Though those are both true.

"I was thinking of taking a walk on the beach."

My shoulders drop. I feel like I can breathe again. A beach walk is safe territory. The Cove is beautiful but busy this time of the year. Maybe we could grab ice cream at Grant's shop— Sweet Harmony. Alex would like the place, it has a touch of city sophistication, and he makes all the flavors in store.

My mind is running away with imagined plans for the evening—safe, no-one-gets-their-feelings-hurt plans—when Alex speaks again. "Do you know of a quieter beach that isn't so busy?"

"I do." I say the words before I can think better of them. Before I can remember the danger of getting too close to this beautiful, passionate woman. Dean Markham hasn't forgotten. He'd torn into me after the farmer's market and growled when I'd explained Grammie Rae's invitation. And now he's inserted himself as a judge for the first time in the Bonanza's history—just to keep an eye on us.

"Any interest in spending the evening with me?" Alex asks as if it's even a question. As if I'd rather go home or to Paris or to the moon if spending the night with her was an alternative option.

I take a deep breath. One more day with Alex Sinclair, then she'll be out of my life forever. Dean has nothing to worry about. And I'm just going to make the most of the day we have left. "That sounds great."

Alex

Maybe it's the thrill of actually milking a cow. Or the wild emotional rollercoaster of losing a small-town cooking competition—something Missy will probably never let me live down. Whatever it was, I knew the night couldn't end yet.

Now I'm walking hand-in-hand with Ethan along a stretch of lonely beach as stars slowly dot the twilight sky. In overalls. Alex, a few months ago, would be appalled. Well, not over the man I'm holding hands with—he is objectively gorgeous. But the rest of the situation? Absolutely appalled.

I find that I don't care what old-Alex might think. I'm starting to believe she wasn't happy. Maybe she never has been. I've spent so much of my life surviving, doing the things that had to happen, that I'd forgotten to slow down and consider if I was living the life I actually wanted. Magnolia Cove slowed me down, turned my days into meditations on buttercream and thoughtful morning walks on cobblestone roads.

"You're quiet," Ethan says.

My fingers tighten on his hand. I can't share the thoughts swirling through me because dreams are wonderful, but we all must wake up. "I have to leave soon."

It must come out sadder than I intended because Ethan stops walking and looks at me. Really looks at me. The wind whispers through his curls, and the evening's blue light softens the planes of his face. I shiver, not from the breeze, but from the intimacy of his look. To feel the full weight of Ethan Hart's attention is dizzying.

"Do you want to sit?" he asks.

I nod, and we walk over to a sun-bleached driftwood log, settling down side by side. I rest my head against his shoulder, and he tucks an arm around me as if this is the most natural thing in the world. As if we've done this a hundred times and we'll do it a hundred more. But neither is true.

"My life is in New York."

He presses a kiss to the top of my head and sighs, the warmth of his breath making me shiver. "And mine is here at the Whisk."

Neither of us speaks for a long time. Waves crash across the shore, and sandpipers leap forward then scuttle back over the wet sand, leaving their prints behind them. It's peaceful—the lonely sea, the darkening sky, the surety of Ethan's arm around my shoulders.

If he knew the article I'd started writing, he wouldn't touch me. I can imagine the hurt flashing across his pale blue eyes, the way his brow would furrow. I can see Zoe frowning. Rachel propping her hands on her hips, her lips twisting into a scowl. It's like all of Magnolia Cove is watching me, waiting for what I might say about them.

The last time I spoke with Vivian, I'd soft-pitched the idea of writing an actual feature about the Whisk. She'd laughed. I don't know why I expected more.

Maybe I won't write it. Maybe I won't even return to *Gastronomy Eats* at all. Even thinking that thought has my throat tightening. It's a steady paycheck, a retirement plan with employer contributions, a potential raise. It's certainty in a chaotic world. I tremble, and Ethan pulls me closer.

This—he—feels like certainty, too. Ethan feels like home. Meeting him was like wandering through the woods for what seemed like a lifetime, only to stumble upon a cozy cottage with a soft bed and a well-stocked pantry, where everything just fit.

It's as if neither of us can find the right words. Our feelings are too big to wrap in vowels and consonants. The silence between us stretches, but then a memory of Missy breaks through the stillness. "I'm sure my sister misses me. Or at least the food I usually bring home. She can't cook grilled cheese without setting something on fire. She's probably surviving on some crappy three-dollar hamburgers."

Ethan laughs softly. "Hey, I like crappy, cheap hamburgers."

"Tell me you're lying," I say, raising an eyebrow. "The great baker, Ethan Hart, who special-orders fifty-dollar vanilla extract, could actually be caught eating fast food?"

"Sure could." His grin is slow and easy, and before I can stop myself, I find myself moving closer. He shifts, and now every inch of us is touching, from chest to knee.

My heart races again, and I'm back to thinking impossible things—life-upending, world-shifting things. "I haven't seen any food chains in Magnolia Cove."

"Nope, you won't. Can't find that here." His voice drops, eyes drifting toward the sea, the water stretching between us and the rest of the world. There's love in his tone, but also something more—a bitterness, a weight I can't quite place. It's not his family, because his dad's here too, and they seem close. Whatever it is, it feels too personal, too tied to this place, for me to ask about it now. Especially when I'm about to walk out of his life.

"Tell me something," I say, blurting it out before I can stop myself. "Something about you I don't know yet."

Ethan's thumb brushes across the strap of my overalls, slowly, his touch sending a shiver down my spine. "Hmm... Did you know I'm terrified of heights?"

I turn my face to look at him, eyebrow raised. "Really? But you're so... tall."

He grins, dimples appearing. "Height doesn't matter when you're hanging off the side of a cliff, trust me. Learned that the hard way on a disastrous camping trip in college. Okay, your turn. Tell me something I don't know about you."

I run my fingernail along the rough surface of the log beside me, a small shell wedged into a groove. I try, and fail, to dislodge it. Should I tell him that I'm planning to write an article that could embarrass him? Or that I'm considering not writing it at all, risking my job in the process? The indecision roils inside me, like a boat caught in a storm. I take a deep breath, deciding to be honest, to share something I've only told Tish. "I... I have a food blog. Or, I did. I haven't updated it in years, but it's still out there."

Ethan pauses, his thumb stalling. "Really? What's it called?"

"*Tell Me Something Sweet.*" Heat rushes to my cheeks, and I tuck myself closer to him. "It was my passion project in college. I wrote about hidden gem bakeries, family recipes, the stories behind different desserts. But then I became responsible for my sister, put all my energy into landing the job at *Gastronomy*..."

"And had to give up your dream?" Ethan's voice is soft, his words almost a whisper.

I nod, the weight of it sinking deep into my chest. "Yeah."

The tight spot in my throat returns, and my eyes prick. I can't cry here in front of this man over decisions made years ago. I take a breath of the brackish air. "It was the smart choice, the only one, really. I had to focus on my career, work twice as hard as anyone to build my reputation if I planned to make it work and support myself and Missy."

"It's funny, I thought you were doing exactly the thing you love."

"I am." Aren't I? Or maybe I'm not. Maybe I've found the shadow of the thing I actually love that pays me the most. I remember my disregarded article on Vivian's desk—the hand-lettered title I'd placed on it. The story that will now never see the light of publication. "I have to do what pays me, not just what interests me."

The words taste hollow, but I say them anyway. It's what I was raised to believe—what I watched my mother live by. She used to paint, once. Beautiful, sweeping landscapes, golden light catching on the edges of the brushstrokes. I still remember the smell of oil paint clinging to her, how she'd hum while she worked. But she stopped. There wasn't time between double shifts and keeping everything running after Dad was gone. Passion is a luxury; responsibility isn't.

I press my lips together and shake the memory off. Ethan wouldn't understand. He built a life out of the thing he loves. But not all of us get that choice.

Ethan swipes hair that's blown into my face away and smiles down at me. "And that is how you ended up stuck traveling to Magnolia Cove to write about a kitschy bakery with magical, rainbow marketing."

A laugh bursts from me, and he joins in. He doesn't move his hands from my cheeks. His calluses scrape against my skin, and I stop breathing, only wanting to focus on his touch, on the intensity of his gaze.

"It's not too late, you know," he whispers. "To chase your dreams."

But it is. Missy is the one who gets to follow her heart now. Once she moves out, I might rekindle the blog. I could infuse it with my name, my notoriety, if *Gastronomy Eats* would allow the indulgence. They might not. I'd signed a pretty hefty non-compete with my contract, one that keeps my voice tethered to their brand.

"And you?" I ask instead of answering. "Any unfulfilled dreams hiding behind that firefighter facade?"

He smirks, but it feels almost sad, and his hands drop away from me. "I always wanted to travel more. See the great bakeries of the world, learn techniques from different cultures. But..." He gestures vaguely. "I made a home here instead."

And created a bakery he's poured all his passion, studying, and love into. A bakery I'm about to shatter in my article. It won't hurt his bottom line—I doubt many people who frequent the Whisk read *Gastronomy Eats*. But I know Ethan. It will break something within him.

I reach for his hand, needing the connection. "If you ever decide to take that world tour, call me. I know all the best hidden gems in New York and a few other places as well. Maybe our travels might match up at some point."

Ethan smiles, but there's a sadness in his eyes that makes my chest ache. "I'd like that," he breathes.

We sit in silence as darkness drapes across the sky, and thousands of stars glisten to life over it. I lean in closer to Ethan and rest my head on his shoulder again. Something about this feels so right. "I'm going to miss this," I whisper.

Ethan's arm tightens around me, and he presses a kiss to the top of my head. "Me too."

As night falls, I reluctantly stand, not quite ready for the evening to end. Ethan turns toward the twinkling lights of Magnolia Cove, the beacon calling us back. Then he looks up at the moon. It's nearly full, only a small sliver missing. He hasn't released my hand, and I can't will myself to move away from him. When he looks back down at me, there's such a serious expression on his face, it causes my stomach to swoop.

"I have a cottage close to here," he says, his voice dancing with the wind.

My breath catches in my throat. I wait for him to continue wherever he's going with this, but he only stares at me in such an intense way that it's like I've stumbled into the woods and got caught in a stare-down with a predator. I shiver, but finally sputter out, "I'm sure it's lovely."

"Would you like to see it?" It's like he's fighting himself over saying the words. Like he knows he shouldn't. He must not be much of a one-night-stand kind of guy.

The waves roar behind us, and tension swirls in the limited space between our bodies. I want to close that gap, taste his lips again. I've let work relationships become less professional before—Tish became my best friend after I wrote an article about her. But never this unprofessional.

I should find a way to graciously say no. Make it about me and not him. But staring up into the depths of his eyes as the breeze tangles my hair forward so it brushes his skin, I can't.

"I would like that," I whisper.

Ethan's shoulders drop with a breath. He reaches out and cups my cheek with his hand, then leans in and kisses me quick and soft. It's over before it begins, and I'm left breathless, wanting more as I follow him up the beach, then toward a path.

When we turn a corner, hundreds of beach cottages appear, dotting the shore like shells. These are clearly residential homes and not vacation rentals. The aged wood and personalized touches speak of permanent homes.

"I didn't know this neighborhood was here," I say.

Ethan's hand tightens on mine. "This is where most of the long-term residents in Magnolia Cove live. Zoe and Mia's cottage is just over there, and Rachel has a place just down the lane. It's a little community within the community." He nods ahead of us. "This one's mine."

It's a navy cottage with worn ivory shutters on the far side of the beach, like it's meant to stand alone. A pair of rocking chairs sit on the porch facing a table with a chessboard set up for a game.

Ethan walks up and opens the door—no locks once again—then clicks on a lamp so it glows over the interior as I step inside. He shuts the door while I take it all in.

A leather couch faces a small fireplace, a handmade quilt draped over its back. Bookshelves line one wall, crammed with cookbooks and hundreds of novels. Bookmarks and what appears to be notated papers stick out of dozens of them.

The kitchen juts off the living area as if it's an afterthought, the space small. Despite that, I feel like a moth drawn to it. Copper pots hang from a rack, and a sourdough starter (name-free) sits on a counter next to a bowl of fresh tomatoes—the same varieties I'd seen at his father's farmer's market stall.

A small hallway leads off, presumably to the bathroom and a couple of bedrooms. My stomach clenches.

Ethan clears his throat. He's standing awkwardly by the door, hands shoved into his pockets. "So, um, this is home sweet home."

"I love it," I say, and I mean it.

He walks over to me. I stare up at him, at this man who has captivated me in such a short time. His eyes search mine, and there's a vulnerability about him, standing here surrounded by his treasures.

"Alex," he says softly, "I know you're leaving soon, and I don't want to complicate things, but..." He reaches up and slides hair behind my ear. My skin prickles, and heat builds in my body. Things are already complicated. I'm already spending half my days daydreaming about forever, and if I can't have that, I at least want tonight.

I push up on my tiptoes and kiss him. What begins as a

gentle parting of lips turns urgent. My arms wrap around his neck, and I pull him closer to me, tracing my fingers into his curls. His body tucks around mine, every firm inch of muscle I've admired as he kneaded dough and lifted heavy sacks of flour pressing against me. His hands glide down my back, grip my hips, and pull me flush against him.

A moan escapes my lips as Ethan's mouth trails down my neck, his stubble grazing my sensitive skin. My fingers fumble to undo the buttons of his shirt, desperate to feel more. He pulls back, his eyes searching mine. "Are you sure?"

His voice is rough, and it makes my heart race. I capture his lips and pour every drop of longing I've felt in the past weeks into it. "I'm sure," I breathe against his mouth.

Ethan curls his hands around my hips, then lifts me effort-lessly. I squeal in surprise but wrap my legs around his waist. He carries me down the hall into the dark bedroom. Only the moon's light spills over the quilt-covered bed, and I exhale slowly as he places me on it.

He stares at me, brushes hair behind my shoulder, then lets his fingers trace down my arm. I shiver at the touch, at the change in intensity.

Ethan stands over me, his silhouette bathed in moonlight, rising and falling with his heavy breaths. He reaches out and traces his thumb along my collarbone, his eyes never leaving mine. Our ragged breaths mingle with the waves crashing in the distance.

Slowly, as if savoring the moment, Ethan kneels before me. His hands glide down to my hips, then slide back up to my waist, pausing as though he's giving me every chance to stop him. The weight of his gaze feels like a promise, and I arch toward him, craving more.

His fingers deftly pull my shirt off. The air kisses me with a cool breath. Ethan groans, then trails his hands over my newly exposed skin.

I close my eyes and imagine those hands kneading dough and piping frosting. Their finesse and gentleness. I want him to touch me everywhere. I gasp when his lips follow the path his hands have trailed, pressing slow, deliberate kisses along my collarbone.

I reach for him and pull his shirt off his shoulders, revealing the hard planes of his chest, muscles flexing as he moves. His body is warm and solid, grounding me as his hands roam, teasing slowly, fingers slipping under remaining fabric.

"Alex," he murmurs against my skin, voice husky. "I've wanted this... wanted you..." His confession hangs in the air between us, a raw truth.

"I've wanted this too," I whisper. Perhaps since the moment I saw his picture in the magazine. Now Ethan Hart has his mouth everywhere on me. His tongue traces down my stomach, then pauses as he nips at the skin, eliciting another gasp. He kisses me again, deeper and more desperate, as though he knows this is our one chance, and he doesn't mean to waste it.

He slides his hands down my skin, the rough pads of his fingers gliding over my thighs. I shudder but arch to meet his touch.

He pauses for a heartbeat, his forehead resting against mine as we both catch our breath. "I need you to tell me if it's too much... if you want me to stop," he whispers against my cheek.

I shake my head, breathless still. "Don't stop. Oh god, Ethan, please don't stop."

He slides his hand farther up, slow and torturous, as his other arm braces above me. His touch is reverent, as though he's savoring each moment, each moan he pulls from me, each time I rise to meet his body with mine.

I sense more than see him reaching for the nightstand. The heat between us builds, layer by layer. Ethan takes his time, peeling away clothing, then kissing and exploring each new space. Every touch feels like things he can't voice, promises he wishes he could make. There are words I want to say as well. Words I can't.

They don't seem to matter in the quiet of his cottage, under the light of the moon. It feels like the world has faded, leaving just us, our breaths, our flesh gliding together, and the pull of everything unsaid finding its release differently.

Ethan kisses my shoulder and whispers against it. "Stay tonight?"

"Okay," I find myself answering.

And when he, half asleep, mumbles that if I'll still be here for the weekend, he has one more Magnolia Cove experience he'd like to show me, I find myself agreeing. And I'm too drowsy and happy to worry about how I'm going to make that work.

If Ethan Hart asks me to stay forever, I might just say yes.

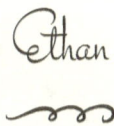

Ethan

The coffee maker gurgles softly as pre-dawn light creeps through my kitchen windows. I'm standing in pajama pants, bare feet pressed against the cool wood floor, staring out at the ocean.

My internal clock doesn't care that I'm not opening the Whisk. Though today, waking early feels like a gift. It gives me time to process the impossible: Alexandra Sinclair is asleep in my bed.

I take a sip of coffee and let memories of last night wash over me. Her skin glowing in moonlight. The way she said my name. How desperately I wanted to show her every part of myself—even the parts that terrify others. But mostly, I remember the peace. Despite the nearly full moon hanging heavy in the sky, despite my magic usually running wild during lunar events, everything inside me had been still. Like somehow, she anchored me—held the chaos at bay without even trying.

Setting my mug down, I walk back to the bedroom doorway. She's curled on her side, my quilt tucked around her waist, her bare shoulder gleaming in the silvery pre-dawn light.

Her hair spreads across my pillow like spun gold, and her face... God, her face in sleep. All the sharp edges of the renowned food critic have melted away, leaving something soft and precious.

She looks like she belongs here. Like she's meant to be tangled in my sheets every morning, sharing coffee and lazy kisses before the rest of the world wakes.

The thought sends an ache through my chest. Because she can't stay. Dean lives three cottages down, and if word gets back to the Council that I'm getting too close to a non-magical human again... I close my eyes, remembering Sarah's terror, my magic overwhelming me, the chaos that followed. I won't risk Alex like that. Won't risk the entire community's safety for my own desires.

But standing here, watching her sleep, it's hard to remember all the reasons this is dangerous. She shifts, and my quilt slips lower, revealing the delicate slope of her shoulder, the smooth line of her collarbone. My fingers itch to trace constellations between the freckles dusting her shoulders. To wake her with gentle kisses and whispered promises.

The coffee maker gives a final sputter in the background, breaking my reverie. I should rouse her soon, get her back to the B&B before the town stirs. Before Dean does his morning check-in. Before—

"You're thinking too loud," Alex mumbles against the pillow.

My heart stutters. She blinks sleepily at me and everything else falls away. The Council, Dean, my own fears—none of it matters when she's looking at me like that.

"Sorry," I whisper. "Habit. Baker's hours and all that."

She stretches, catlike and graceful, before sitting up. The quilt pools around her waist, and my mouth goes dry. "Tell me you at least made enough coffee for two?"

I smirk. "Stay in bed. I'll bring you some."

I push off the doorframe and head to the kitchen, the scent of fresh brew filling the air. It's automatic, the way I move through the motions—pouring, placing the mug just the way I like it—except this time, it's not for me.

When I return, she's sitting up, the quilt pooled around her. I hand her the cup, and she takes a slow sip, then sighs in appreciation. "You make a strong case for the merits of small-town coastal life."

"That's just the Sumatra Mandheling speaking," I say, but my chest tightens at her words. Because god, do I wish it was true. Wish I could give her mornings like this stretched out endlessly—strong coffee and ocean breezes, lazy kisses and shared silence. Wish I could show her the real magic of small-town life, not just the curated version we present to tourists.

When I glance at the clock, reality sets back in. Dean rises early. Always has. And the way he watches me, especially during lunar events...

"Actually," I say, hating myself a little, "maybe we should get you back to the B&B before too many people are up and about."

Her expression falls for just a moment before she covers it with a smirk. "Ashamed to be seen with me, Chief?"

"Never." The word comes out fiercer than I intended, because it's true. If anything, I'm not worthy of being seen with her. "It's just..."

"A small town where people talk?" She finishes for me, her tone knowing. "And certain people might not approve?"

I run a hand through my hair, probably making it even messier than sleep left it. "Something like that."

She thinks this is just about small-town gossip, about people talking over their morning pastries at the Whisk. But all I can think about is Dean, how he'd blow a gasket if he found out about this—no matter how carefully I'd kept my magic in check last night, no matter that the full moon hadn't affected me at all around her. Some things he'd never understand, and Alex Sinclair in my bed is definitely one of them.

She studies me for a long moment, and I have to fight the urge to look away. Sometimes her gaze is so sharp, so perceptive, I worry she'll see right through me. See the magic thrumming beneath my skin, the darkness lurking in my bones.

Finally, she rises from the bed and walks over to where I'd left a button-down draped over the back of a chair. My breath catches as she slips it on—the hem falling to mid-thigh. Somehow seeing her in my clothes is more intimate than seeing her wearing nothing at all.

She pads over and rises on her tiptoes to press a soft kiss to my lips. "Do I have time to finish my coffee?"

"Of course." I glance toward the window, where the sky is still deep indigo, the first hints of dawn barely creeping over the horizon. Magnolia Cove is still asleep—for now.

"Alright, Mr. Hart. But you owe me breakfast another time."

The promise in her words makes my chest ache. Because there shouldn't be another time. I shouldn't even be allowing this time. But as she slips her hand into mine, warm and sure, I can't bring myself to tell her that.

"You're cute when you're worried," she whispers against my mouth.

I wrap my arms around her waist, pulling her closer. "And you're beautiful when you're asleep."

"I am?" Her voice is soft, almost shy—so different from her usual confident tone. Her fingers trace patterns on my chest, and I wonder if she can feel my heart thundering beneath them.

"You are." I brush hair back from her face, letting my thumb graze her cheek. "The way the moonlight plays across your skin. How peaceful you look." I pause, realizing how that must sound. "I'm sorry. That's creepy, isn't it?"

But Alex just smiles, her eyes crinkling at the corners. "No, it's sweet. Though I'm surprised you could see me at all, given how thoroughly I stole all your blankets."

"I noticed that too." A laugh spills from me as I remember how I'd found her completely cocooned in my quilt. "I didn't take you for a blanket thief."

"There's a lot you don't know about me."

Her tone is teasing, but something in her eyes makes my breath catch. Because I want to know everything about her—every habit, every quirk, every dream she's ever had. But I can't reciprocate that openness. Can't let her truly know me.

The realization sits like lead in my stomach. Here she is, vulnerable and trusting in my arms, while I hide the most fundamental truths about myself.

We dress quickly, hands brushing, fingers lingering—stealing every touch we can in the quiet between us. A whispered laugh, the accidental graze of her lips against my shoulder, the warmth of her palm on my back.

And then, too soon, it's time to go. I pour her a to-go cup of coffee, pressing it into her hands like it's the only thing I can give her.

"Wait," I say as she reaches for the door handle. "Let me check first."

Alex raises an eyebrow as I peer through the front window like a teenager sneaking out past curfew. "You realize I've been staying at a B&B in town for weeks? People have seen me before."

"Yes, but..." Not like this. Not with morning-mussed hair and wrinkled clothing, practically glowing from a night of... I clear my throat. "Just humor me?"

Her laugh is soft and fond. "Whatever you say, Chief."

The coast looks clear. Dean's cottage shows no signs of life, though that doesn't mean much. The man moves like a shadow when he wants. I guide Alex onto the porch, wincing at every creak of the old boards beneath our feet.

We make it down the steps and halfway up the beach path before I relax. Maybe we'll actually pull this off—

"Well, well, well!"

We freeze. The voice carries with it such delighted mischief that I don't even need to turn around to know who it is. Alex's hand tightens in mine as Zoe practically bounces into view, her purple hair wild in its morning bun, grinning like she's just discovered the secret ingredient to my banana bread recipe.

"Aren't you supposed to be opening the Whisk?" I try to keep my voice casual, but it comes out more like a plea.

"Aren't you supposed to be maintaining professional boundaries with our resident food critic?" She wiggles her eyebrows at me before shifting her grin to Alex, mischief written all over her face. "Those overalls are looking a bit more wrinkled than they did at the Bonanza, City Girl. Late night?"

Alex bursts out laughing, but my face burns. "Zoe—"

"Don't worry, Boss." She mimes zipping her lips, but her eyes dance with unholy glee. "Though work on your sneaking skills. Even Mrs. Delehay's Pomeranian is stealthier than you two." She cocks an eyebrow. "I thought city girls had mastered the art of the stealthy exit."

I think I actually feel the color drain from my face. But Alex just shrugs. "Can't say I have much experience with sneaking out. But I guess there's a first time for everything."

The implication of Alex's words hits me like a physical force. She doesn't do this—doesn't spend nights with men she barely knows, doesn't sneak out of their homes in wrinkled clothes. The gravity of that settles in my chest, warm and terrifying all at once. Because this isn't casual for her either. Last night wasn't just about desire or convenience. But if she's all in, even unknowingly, then I'm putting her at risk.

And that makes everything more complicated. More dangerous. More precious.

Zoe must read something in my expression because her teasing smile softens into something gentler. "Well, your secret's safe with me, Sugar." She backs away, but can't quite resist adding, "Though Mia's going to groan when I tell her I was right."

"Right about what?" Alex asks.

"Nothing!" I say quickly, probably too quickly judging by both women's knowing looks.

"I've got to run." Zoe shoots me another grin—a grin that says tomorrow at work, she will hound me until I either confess every detail or beg for mercy. Probably both. "Some of us actually have to work today. Try not to look too happy when Dean does his morning rounds, Boss."

She disappears around the corner, leaving us in the pre-dawn quiet. Alex's hand is still warm in mine, and when I look down at her, the soft light catching in her eyes steals my breath. The sun is just beginning to paint the horizon in watercolor pinks and golds, and she looks... right. Like she belongs here, walking these familiar streets with me, as if we've done this a hundred mornings before.

"Come on," I say, my voice rougher than intended. "Let's get you back."

But as we walk, our footsteps falling into a peaceful rhythm, I can't help but wonder if I'm making a mistake. If I'm already in too deep. The Council's rules exist for a reason —I know that better than most. One slip of control, one moment of weakness, and I could destroy everything. Not just the town's secrets, but Alex's trust. Her safety. Her smile when she looks at me like I'm something precious instead of something to fear.

And yet.

And yet, when her fingers tighten around mine, when she

leans into me as a cool morning breeze sweeps in from the ocean, I can't bring myself to pull away. Maybe that makes me selfish. Maybe it makes me dangerous.

Or maybe it makes me human. The most human I've felt since the Council bound my magic and banished me here.

Dean would say I'm falling into old patterns, taking risks I can't afford. But as Alex's thumb traces absent patterns against my palm, as the seabirds wheel overhead and the town slowly stirs to life around us, I realize something that terrifies me more than any Council decree:

I don't care.

I don't care about the rules or the risks or the consequences. Because for the first time since I arrived in Magnolia Cove, I feel like I'm exactly where I'm supposed to be. Walking these quiet streets with a woman who makes me forget about the darkness beneath my skin. Who makes me believe that maybe, just maybe, I deserve a chance at something real.

Even if that chance might cost me everything.

Alex

Papers are scattered everywhere on my desk. Golden sunlight streams past the floral-embroidered curtains in my B&B room. I'm trying to focus on my articles that are due and not think about the message from Vivian, who wants us to have a call. I'm sure my editor is going to rail into me about extending my stay so long despite not yet missing a deadline. According to her message, I had skipped a crucial meeting.

I cringe, but the feeling flits away. Because my mind is stuck on Ethan Hart.

Ethan patiently working with Jas on a new project.

Ethan running around the farm, his t-shirt showing every muscle.

Ethan bare and wrapped around me as the ocean roared in the distance, asking me to stay just a little longer.

Missy's voice over the phone's speaker pulls me out of my reverie. Her sing-song tone echoes around the room. "In Music History this week, we're discussing the evolution of the cello's role in orchestras. I can't believe it was once considered a bit player."

I chuckle—I know what it feels like to realize something

you love was once undervalued. Sourdough bread was once the food of peasants while the upper class dined on refined white loaves. Now the tables have turned, and epicureans consider the hearty, flavorful sourdough haute cuisine. I'm wanting to ask Missy if she's fed our starter, but I suspect I already know the disappointing answer to that. "And how's practice going for the recital?"

"Ugh, don't remind me." She groans, and I can imagine her flinging herself into the oversized bean bag in her room. "I'm practically dreaming in Dvořák at this point. You'll be back in time for that, right?"

"Of course," I say, because of course I will. Even if a part of me wilts at the idea of returning to city life and its demands.

As Missy launches into a detailed description of the second movement of the song she's working on, I open mail I've had directed here. It takes forever to get to Magnolia Cove through the ferry. One in particular has my attention. The label is from my old journalism mentor, Jack. He doesn't write about food, but he has a nose for a good story. Which is exactly why I reached out to him shortly after arriving in Magnolia Cove to see if he could find information I couldn't. I rip open the manila envelope. A collection of newspaper clippings spills onto my desk.

"Hang on a sec, Missy."

"Everything okay?" My fingers freeze on an article with a familiar face staring back at me—Ethan's face.

"Yeah, I'm fine, just work stuff buzzing in, and I need to take care of it. Try to eat something with some fiber in it today, for my sake, please?"

She laughs. "No promises. Love you, sis."

"Love you too."

The phone line clicks, but I don't move. I'm staring at the article, at clear blue eyes turned gray in newsprint, haunted and wild in a way I've never seen before.

With trembling hands, I lift the clipped article and read:

"Late last night, several eyewitnesses reported unusual disturbances in the downtown area, including smashed vehicle windshields and damaged storefronts. Local resident Ethan Hart was seen in the vicinity shortly before the incident, appearing disoriented and agitated. He fled the scene but was later apprehended by police. Officials urge the public to remain calm, stating there is no ongoing threat to the community."

The article describes a scene of destruction: damaged vehicles, knife-slashed building awnings, shattered windows, and terrified onlookers. It paints a picture of Ethan that's completely at odds with the gentle baker I know.

My mind races, stretching, attempting to find any evidence that this article could be true. Ethan handing out free treats to local kids. His passionate stories about his grandmotherly neighbor in France. The way his eyes crinkle when he laughs at my terrible puns. The warmth of his arms around me just last night...

No, this doesn't make sense. It can't be the same Ethan. But the picture—it's Ethan, down to the thick jawline and messy curls. Younger, with shadowed eyes and thin lips I've never seen on him before. But definitely him.

Air blows from the vent, sending a gust down the back of my silk top and making me shiver. Other vacationers in the inn walk in, shutting the front door with a thud. Birds whistle outside my cracked window. Sunlight undulates over the papers. I remain frozen, my gaze fixed on Ethan's vacant stare.

I force myself to flip through the other documents Jack sent. Most are innocuous—recent articles about The Whimsical Whisk and the odd recipe Ethan had submitted to publications. But there's another clipping that has me catching my breath. The headline reads: 'Local Woman Speaks Out: The Ethan Hart I Knew.'

My hands tremble as I read.

In an exclusive interview, Sarah Callahan, ex-girlfriend of Ethan Hart, shares her experience with the man at the center of last month's bizarre incident. "Ethan was... intense," Callahan stated. "He could be the sweetest person one moment, then become someone else entirely the next. I want to say these charges surprise me, but unfortunately, they don't."

The pit in my stomach grows. There's something here—a story that I need to know about. I should have already known about it. I probably should have figured it out before I wandered around Ethan's cottage this morning wearing one of his button-downs and drinking coffee from one of his Nan's mugs.

I need answers. Now.

Grabbing my linen jacket, I rush out of the B&B and head toward The Whimsical Whisk. I'd planned to keep my distance, catch up on work, and try to ensure Vivian doesn't fire me. But if I'm honest, it wasn't just about deadlines. Distance feels safer—less dangerous. Because the closer I get to Ethan, the harder it is to pretend I can leave without looking back.

Magnolia Cove is just as picturesque as it seemed on the first day—squirrels jump between the massive trees on Main Street, and the windows gleam just as brightly. Mrs. Delehay waves at me from across the street, beaming, no doubt still thinking about the croquembouche Ethan made her—flawless, golden, and stacked as effortlessly as if he were showing off. I grin at Mia, who stacks books for a new display in the bookstore window. Everything feels normal, but internally my world has tilted.

Ethan has been hiding something. I've felt it from the beginning, but I never would have guessed it was a criminal past.

The Whisk's teal awning comes into view, and I slow down, taking a few breaths. I need to give Ethan the benefit of the doubt. For all I know, the article could be a case of false allegations. I've seen nothing in his actions that remotely resemble the newspaper article.

I take another step, then stop. Voices are coming from the alley—gruff and terse. I take a peek around the corner, then jump back so quickly that I land flat against the brick wall. I recognize Ethan immediately. His tall frame and broad shoulders are unmistakable even in the shadows. Dean stands across from him, his chin raised, hands fisted.

Sliding up to the edge of the corner, I press myself against the wall, straining to hear their conversation. My heart pounds so loudly I'm afraid they'll hear it.

"...can't keep doing this, Ethan." Dean's voice is low and intense. "You're skating on thin ice as it is."

"I know. I'm willing to concede that you're right for once. But Alex is different. She's not like—"

"Not like the last one?" Dean cuts in sharply. "I'm sure that's what you thought with the other girl as well, and look at how that turned out. The Council had to work overtime to clean up that mess."

A chill runs down my spine. Council? Clean up? What the hell have I stumbled into? Suddenly, I'm struggling to remember the warmth of Ethan's arms around me.

Dean's voice softens slightly. "Look, I get it. But you need to think with your head for once. We can't afford another incident, and you know what the consequences are for you if something happens."

When Ethan finally speaks again, his voice is full of defeat. It makes me want to throw all my suspicions aside and jump forward to defend him. "I know. I understand. I just... I wish things could be different. I wish I could tell her everything."

"You can't," Dean says firmly, all gentleness gone. "Not

unless you want to risk everything—for all of us. Remember what's at stake here. It's not just about you."

I lean around the corner to see Ethan. He's slumped, defeated, his face lowered. It makes me want to run to him. Though now, I'm not sure I even know him. A twig snaps under my foot, and I freeze.

Ethan's head jerks up. For a moment, I could swear his eyes glow in the dim light, like a cat's catching a streetlamp's reflection. But that's impossible. My heart hammers against my ribs, so hard it's painful.

"We should go inside," Dean mutters, and the two men disappear through the bakery's back door.

I lean against the wall as though it might hold me up, my mind whirling. The Ethan in that article, the one Dean was warning about—it doesn't match the man I thought I knew. Or does it? Those gentle hands that caressed me so tenderly last night—are they the same ones that caused destruction and harm?

I don't know who Ethan Hart is, really. Or what secrets Magnolia Cove is harboring.

With more questions than answers, I walk back up the path toward the B&B. The warmth and joy I felt with Ethan —the thing that made me want to run away from my life and start over with him here—has been replaced by a cold, gnawing doubt.

I'm missing something crucial. Something that would help this all make sense. But one thing is clear—there's more to Ethan Hart than meets the eye.

I pause on the B&B's porch. A Magnolia tree shudders in the wind, its dark, glossy leaves glimmering. I have two more nights left on the island, then I leave for the real world. For real this time. But I can't go my entire life without knowing the story here. If I only have hours left, I'm going to use them to discover whatever secret is hiding behind Magnolia Cove's picture-perfect facade.

* * *

Somehow, the Magnolia Cove Library smells like cinnamon. The entire town seems to hold the scents of a comforting grandmother's house. The library even has stained-glass windows that allow softly glowing, colorful light to dance in patterns on the rug.

I've walked past this place a dozen times, meaning to stop in, but it's only now, with questions tugging at my heart, that I finally do.

I approach the front desk, where a librarian with her hair French-braided and a cardigan punctuated with colorful pins sits typing at a computer. The pins say things like 'prose before bros' and 'I like big books and I cannot lie.'

I'm smiling when she turns toward me.

"Nice pins."

"Thanks. I make them myself."

"You could give the New York City librarians some ideas."

The woman's smile widens, and she looks me up and down. "New York City, huh? You must be Alex Sinclair. I'm Rihanna. Zoe has told me all about you."

"She's probably made me sound more colorful than I actually am."

Rihanna snorts. "She keeps us on our toes, that one."

There's that "us" again. I've noticed the citizens of Magnolia Cove speak about themselves collectively—like they're more than just neighbors. Dean's conversation with Ethan runs through my mind once more. There's some council that's watching Ethan but also looking out for him. It's like the answer I'm searching for is right in front of my eyes, but there's a mirage keeping me from seeing it.

"I was wondering if you have an archive section about Magnolia Cove's history that I could access?"

Rihanna's expression falters. She jumps up and comes around the desk. "We do, but I'm afraid we had a severe storm a few months back, and they had to lock it up for renovations, so it's closed at the moment. A mess, really. I'm bringing it back up at the council meeting next month. And unfortunately, our non-fiction director, Claire, is out of town. We have other resources available, though. I'll show you what we've got, and you can check back with Claire again next week if you want."

I follow her through the stacks but frown. The bookstore had no history books, the museum didn't possess basic facts about the town's founding, and now the library conveniently lacks the same. As we pass down an aisle, I catch sight of a door labeled 'Local History Archives.' It's locked with a glimmering padlock that glows in the stained-glass light. I stop walking. Light dances around the padlock, twirling into the keyhole and flitting around the metal.

"You okay?" Rihanna frowns at me.

"Ah, yeah. Everything's fine." I offer her a smile, but she doesn't return it. Instead, she marches us forward and begins discussing a book she read for her book club and a music festival she plans to attend next month. She speaks at a rapid clip, like she's attempting to cover something up. But what? There's nothing to hide in a public library.

I spend the next hour poring over what materials I can access, but something's not adding up. There are gaps in the town's records—entire decades missing. What information is available feels completely fake, like someone who's never taken a class in journalistic integrity made it all up.

My stomach growls, reminding me I've skipped not just lunch but dinner. I pack my things and head out, my mind fogged with all my questions. My heart aches for answers that might prove Ethan's innocence. Newspapers run stories with angles all the time. Ethan might have been in the wrong place at the wrong time. Or maybe my heart is just desperate to believe that.

Stepping outside, I'm struck again by how impossibly charming Magnolia Cove is. The flowers along Main Street are as vibrant and in bloom as they were when I first arrived a month ago. A vintage car putters by, its engine purring without a hint of exhaust. A group of boys run down the opposite sidewalk, laughing—Jas among them, I'm glad to see —and when they spill out into the road, the drivers and shop owners only wave at them.

Everything here just seems a touch too idyllic. It's like living inside a Norman Rockwell calendar.

My feet carry me to The Whimsical Whisk before I've made a conscious decision to go there. Zoe's cleaning the display glass, humming some fast-paced tune I don't know.

"Well, well, well," she chirps as she jumps to her feet. "I'm afraid the Bonanza champion isn't here currently, but you look like you could use a pick-me-up, and I know just the thing."

My heart sinks to hear Ethan isn't at the Whisk. I should have known as much, though. He spends Friday afternoons with his father. It hits me how well I've gotten to know him, and yet there are these secrets stretching between us as big as a chasm.

As Zoe bustles behind the counter, I take my usual booth and gather my courage. "Hey, Zoe, can I ask you something?"

She walks out with a muffin that smells of peanut butter, studded with glistening chocolate chips and a dusting of sanding sugar in one hand and a tall glass of milk in the other. My stomach gives a dramatic growl. I've entirely neglected basic needs as I've spent the day trying to find the missing pieces to the puzzle of Magnolia Cove, to the puzzle of Ethan

Hart. Zoe chuckles and nudges the food in my direction, insisting I take a bite before she answers. It melts in my mouth and tastes like sitting before a warm fire.

"Shoot, Sugar. But if it's about Ethan's secret family of circus performers, I'm sworn to secrecy."

"I... wait, what?"

Zoe laughs and points at my food again. I take another bite, fighting back a groan at the flavor's depth, before she replies. "Just keeping you on your toes. Now, what's really on your mind?"

I take a deep breath. "I've been researching the town's history, and... well, I came across some information about Ethan. About an incident in his past. Not here in Magnolia Cove, but in a city somewhere else."

I'm almost certain her smile falters, but her voice sounds the same. "Playing detective, are we? Should have expected that from our initial meeting."

"Zoe, I'm serious." I push the plate forward with the half-eaten muffin still on it. I need actual answers. "This seemed serious and I..." It takes me a moment to gather my courage, and Zoe doesn't interrupt. Instead, she studies me, like she's trying to figure out if I'm worth my credentials. "The thing is, I've come to care about Ethan. I mean, as more than just a story subject. It's unprofessional, I know, but... I really like him, and I'm trying to understand."

Zoe tosses her polishing rag onto the table and sighs as she takes a seat. The intensity is back in her dark eyes, and she doesn't break my gaze as she sits in silence for a moment. She tucks a strand of purple hair behind her ear. "Listen, City Girl, every town's got its skeletons, and every person's got a few of them too. But here's the thing about skeletons—they're a lot less scary if you shine a light on them. You know what I'm saying?"

I think I do. She nudges the plate back toward me, and I

take another small bite. The muffin tastes like everything Ethan bakes—sweetness perfectly balanced with a rich depth, the crumb light and tender. It leaves me more convinced that there's a misunderstanding, that the article didn't have the facts. Journalism, unfortunately, isn't always the most accurate craft.

Sometimes, selling a hot angle matters more, even if it's not true. Like when Vivian laughed about me actually featuring the Whisk. Our job is to sell magazines first, accurate stories second.

"Talk to Ethan." Zoe is, for once, entirely serious. Her tattoos gleam as she crosses her arms, but there's a twinkle in her eyes. "Some stories aren't mine to tell. If you want to know Ethan's past, you should ask him."

"I'm scared," I admit softly. "When I came here, I didn't expect to meet—" I want to say Ethan. I want to say someone who makes me feel alive and seen, something beyond duty, work, and hardship. Instead, I lamely finish with, "all this."

Zoe nods, though, as if she understands. "Love," she says carefully, "has a way of changing everything. The question is, are you ready for that kind of change?"

I feel breathless, the food frozen in my hand. Love? Is that what this feeling is? Does that explain the warmth that spreads through my chest every time I think of Ethan's crooked smile? How I can't read an article without highlighting a recipe technique he'd find interesting? The pulling sensation that's keeping me here on Magnolia Cove, long after my departure date?

I force a smile. "Thanks for dinner, Zoe."

She scowls. "That's barely a snack. You should stop by *The Hungry Gull*. Hazel will feed you something that will actually stick to your ribs." Her nose wrinkles, and her mouth curls into a scowl. "Just don't accept the coffee, no matter what she says."

I laugh and make my way to the door. "So I've heard. And, Zoe? Thanks for the advice, as well."

She only nods, then turns back to her nemesis, the smudged glass, and gets back to work.

I wander almost aimlessly down the street. Ethan will spend the entire evening with his father, then work all day tomorrow. We already have plans to go to a Magnolia Cove summer festival tomorrow evening—an event he wanted me to see. He said there's something more about the island I'll discover there. I'll have to find my bravery and ask Ethan directly about everything at the event.

Zoe implied it wasn't as bad as it seems. I'm willing to have faith that it's true. Tomorrow, I'll get my answers. About Ethan, about this town, about the strange magic that seems to hum in the air here.

More than that, I'll be taking a step toward something I never expected to find. Something that terrifies and thrills me in equal measure.

Love.

I've spent my entire life surviving, but maybe Zoe was right. Maybe I'm ready for a change after all.

Ethan

The last time the Witches and Warlocks Council called an emergency meeting, my entire world tilted on its axis. Now, as I stand beside Dad in the heavily warded council building tucked away beyond the residents' area, the same sense of foreboding crawls up my spine.

The air crackles with tension as Dean takes his place at the head of the gathering. Most of Magnolia Cove's magical adult residents are here, their worried whispers filling the concave room like agitated bees. I scan the crowd, noting the concerned faces of people I've known for years.

"Rihanna Wilder," Dean's voice cuts through the murmurs. "Step forward, please."

Rihanna, her usual cheery demeanor subdued, moves to the center of the room. "Alexandra Sinclair has been asking questions about Magnolia Cove's history," she reports, her voice tight. "She's been digging into areas we... haven't made accessible."

My heart skips a beat at the mention of Alex's name. I think of her curious eyes, the determined set of her jaw when she's onto something. Of course, she's been digging. It's who she is.

"She seems really nice, though," Rihanna adds, glancing at Zoe, who stands beside me. Zoe is glaring, her lips pinched—not at Rihanna, but at the situation. They're close, always in sync, but right now, Zoe is standing firm. She's on my side, and she doesn't like that Rihanna is pushing this up the chain. I want to thank her for protecting Alex for my sake. I want to apologize for dragging her into my trouble. But I already know she'd roll her eyes at that.

Nods and concerned mutters ripple through the crowd. Marcus speaks up next. "She's been nosing around the bookstore too, looking for old records."

"And she's peppered my customers with questions," Hazel chimes in, her usually warm, Southern drawl tinged with worry.

Zoe steps closer to me, and Mia moves in right behind her. "She's just curious about Ethan," Zoe says. "He should have a right to share his own truth with her. I don't think she wants to harm anyone here. She's a food writer, not a detective."

Warmth spreads through my chest, a feeling I almost didn't think I'd ever experience again. When the Council first sentenced me to ten years in Magnolia Cove, it felt like a life sentence. Most residents come and go as they please, free to live as they want. But not me. I was placed here under Dean Markham's watch—one last shot to prove I could keep my magic under control. It was a gilded cage wrapped in charm, but a cage all the same.

At first, I was heartbroken, resigned. I trudged to the island, given a taste of normal life but never allowed the freedom to truly live it.

But time has changed things. I've made friends, like Zoe—people who have my back when the pressure rises, when it feels like the ground beneath me is about to collapse.

Dad stands by my side now, arms crossed, his familiar presence solid and unyielding. He's been here before—standing tall before the council, chin raised, daring them to challenge his son. It didn't matter if I was in the wrong. I was his son, and nothing could change that. His steady support comforts me now, just like it did back then.

"I like the girl," Grammie Rae says, leaning casually against a marble half-wall like it's a vegetable stand, her voice soft but certain. "The magic likes her."

Councilwoman Frome's frown deepens from her seat. "She is not magic-born and doesn't belong here. Every additional day she remains on our island, she threatens to harm us."

Their fear of exposure has always been there, simmering just beneath the surface. It's why we live behind wards, why magical communities like this exist—to stay hidden, to be free without the outside world knowing what we are. Because when humans discover magic, it never ends well. It always leaks. And when it does, it's witches and warlocks left to pick up the pieces—erasing memories, fixing the damage, deleting any trace before it spreads too far.

Magic stirs in me, my claws itching to appear. I take a deep breath, willing myself to stay in control. I've gotten so much better at managing my abilities; I've even spent a night with Alex around the full moon without incident. The memory of her sends a pang into my heart. She'd begged off my offer for a nighttime walk on the beach last night, claiming work, but now I wonder if there was more to it.

Dean's voice pulls me back to the present. "I agree. Alexandra Sinclair poses a grave danger to our community," he declares, his eyes sweeping over everyone. "Our safety must be the paramount concern. If absolutely necessary, we can wipe her memory of everything related to Magnolia Cove and—"

"No." The word tears from my throat, rough and primal.

My body fights against giving in to my magic, every muscle taut with the effort of resisting. "You can't steal her memories."

I want her to keep the memories of me, yes, but more than that, memory magic isn't a perfect science. People have ended up damaged from the effects before. I won't allow Alex to face that risk.

Dean's gaze locks onto me, hard as flint. "We need to be certain she leaves soon, without dangerous information, and with no intention of returning or turning her pen in our direction."

This is my responsibility. She walked into this town because of me. That means it's on me to make sure she walks out of it—whole.

I square my shoulders. "I can make sure that happens."

My heart breaks as the words leave me. Jas' mom gives me a sympathetic look, and it makes me feel ashamed. Ashamed that she still sees good in me, sees me as her son's mentor rather than the man that's put him in danger. Sees my heartache as something worth sympathizing with rather than the monster others in the room are glaring at.

"See that you do." Dean's voice is crisp. "Or we will handle it ourselves. And you, Ethan, will be relocated to a more... secure community."

Dad takes a step forward, but I grab his arm to stop whatever he's about to say or do.

The threat hangs in the air, heavy and suffocating. My mind races. I stand to lose everything—my friendships, my father, the Whisk, Zoe, any connections to the outside world. And Alex. I'm going to lose her, but maybe, just maybe, I can do it in a way that keeps her from getting hurt.

As the meeting disperses, and we walk back out toward the dark sea, Dad claps my shoulder. He says nothing, but I know what goes unspoken. He's at my side no matter what. I clench his fingers and turn down the path. Zoe catches up, Mia with her, and hisses in a whisper at my side. "They can't do this."

"They can and they will, Zo."

"No, we're residents here too. We have a right. We have—"

"No right to hurt others for the sake of me following my heart." I stop walking and look down at Zoe and Mia, the happiest couple I know. The people who have what I've always wanted but will never get to have. "I've done it before, and I won't do it again."

"But you love her, Ethan," Zoe whispers.

She's so serious that, in another context, it would almost be comical. But instead, it only makes my chest ache more, especially as it's emphasized by Mia's sad, wide eyes glistening with tears.

"It doesn't matter," I say finally. The salty, sweet scent of Magnolia Cove fills my lungs. It's the scent of home, of the place I've come to know and love. Now it's tinged with bitterness and loss, but I can't selfishly harm everyone for my desires. I can't allow Alex to get caught up in my troubles, harm her as I've done to another in the past. She's too good for Ethan Hart, was from the moment she stepped her designer shoes on this island. If I tell her the truth about me and she doesn't accept it, they'd have to wipe her memories. I can't risk her harm for my sake.

"What will you do, Ethan?" Mia asks.

I take another deep breath, then let it rush out on the wind. "You heard what Dean said. We need Alex to leave and never want to come back. I'm going to have to break her heart."

Zoe fists her hands and parts her lips, but I shake my head. We all know it's what needs to happen. She grimaces. "What about the Whisk? She might write an article destroying it."

I've had worse dreams die than my renown in the food world. For the longest time, it seemed like my greatest desire, but now everything has changed. I'd give up the Whisk to have Alex. But that's impossible.

"It's not like we'll lose customers over it," I say sadly, turning away from my friends.

A scathing review won't hurt business—if anything, it might drive more people to visit. The only one it would hurt is me.

There's a whispered argument behind me. From what I can catch of their words, Zoe wants to follow me, but Mia says I need space. That's probably what I need—to get away from the town proper, where I can give in to my magic fully. To get away from the place I've poured my heart and dreams into, where I've found purpose and joy, only for it to destroy me in the end, regardless.

I clench my jaw and set myself to my task.

Tomorrow, I'll have to shatter dreams I just realized I had.

Ethan

The moon's light bathes the shore in an ethereal glow, turning the familiar coastline into something out of a fairytale. Walking with Alex's shoulder brushing mine, I feel like I'm living a fantasy. My mind races with the weight of what I have to do tonight, the Council's warning ringing in my ears.

Magic sings through the breeze, thick and potent, as we approach the moon-bathed shore. Hundreds of others have already gathered, spreading out on blankets or perching along rocks. I plan to lead Alex up the cliffside where she can experience the night's wonder without getting too close and realizing things she shouldn't. My initial plan was to bring her here to see the magic, but now I need to hide it from her.

She likely can't see all that I see—the shimmering threads of magic washing in with the waves, the faint glow emanating from the witches' and warlocks' skin as they stand clustered together, the way the very air seems to hum with possibility. Tiny, glistening lights sizzle through the night, flickering and popping like invisible sparklers—someone's subtle magic at play, weaving harmless enchantments into the air. Most people here don't have powerful magic, but they don't need to.

They're here to bask in it, to soak up the warmth of a world where the impossible is just part of the scenery.

"It's so beautiful here," Alex breathes. If only she knew how much magic enhanced Magnolia Cove. That even tourists got a taste of the beauty when they stepped onto the island. Even non-magical humans. Like her.

I force a smile, trying to ignore the voice in my head screaming that Zoe is right. That there has to be another way. "Wait until you see the view from the cliffs," I say as I step in that direction—away from the crowd, away from the truth I can't share.

As we pass the gathering, I catch Dean's eye. His stern gaze follows us, a silent reminder of the threat hanging over my head. The threat to Alex's memories should I fail. I give him a slight nod. I understand what I must do.

"Come on," I say to Alex, "let's head up. The view is incredible."

As we make our way up the winding path, Alex's eyes dart around, taking in every detail. She's observant—it's part of what makes her a talented writer. But tonight, that keen perception could be dangerous.

We reach the top of the cliff, and Alex gasps. The sight never fails to take my breath away, either, even after years of experiencing the summer ritual. The full moon hangs low over the water, its reflection shimmering in broken pieces across the waves. Just beneath the surface, hundreds of moon jellies glow with an otherworldly light.

"Ethan, this is... magical," Alex whispers, her eyes wide and fixed on the sea.

If only she knew how right she was.

A gust of wind picks up, and she steps closer. No one else is around to see, so I tuck an arm over her shoulder. She sighs into my chest, and the bittersweet ache in my heart physically hurts. I think this might be how a heart attack feels.

"Look," I say, pointing to the water. "They're gathering."

More of the luminescent creatures appear, their soft blue glow brightening with each wave's crash. Moon jellies—real, but drawn in by the magic, responding to the energy we channel tonight. They drift like fallen stars just beneath the water's surface, pulsing with the tide, a living reflection of the power humming in the air. It's a magnificent sight, one that even non-magical folks can appreciate. It's also a secret—sacred, really.

We never invite humans to our rituals. This isn't just a celebration; it's how we fuel our magic, syncing ourselves with the pull of the moon, the rhythm of the tide, the energy shifting in the air. We dress it up as a festival, something to enjoy, but it's more than that—it's a way to stay connected, to keep our magic strong.

But Alex isn't just anyone, and if she was going to leave soon, I wanted to give her some magic to take with her. It feels even more important now, since she won't take good memories of me.

Another breeze whips across the cliff's edge, and Alex shudders. I slide my flannel jacket off and tuck it around her shoulders. I hadn't considered how cool it would be up here. "It's getting chilly. Maybe we should head back down."

But Alex doesn't seem to hear. She leans forward, her brow furrowing. "Ethan," she says slowly, "is it just me, or are those jellies... moving in patterns?"

My heart launches into my throat. She's noticing too much. The jellies are indeed moving in intricate but subtle magic-bound patterns. I'd hoped from up here it wouldn't be too obvious. Down on the shore, others will start lighting a bonfire. Magic will be on full display. I hadn't realized she'd pick up on the jellies' gentle dance. "The ocean can make them look like that. We get odd tidal patterns here offshore."

She turns away from the sea, her fingers clasping my jacket

against her neck, but she's frowning. "It seems Magnolia Cove has many oddities I've noticed."

Her voice has become sharp, and my stomach clenches as though she's stabbed me with her words. "What do you mean?" I ask, trying to keep my voice casual.

Alex takes a deep breath. She's forgotten the jellies, which are already dispersing. Distant happy cries ring out from the beach below, but she doesn't seem to notice that either.

"I mean... ever since I arrived here, I've felt like there's something just beyond my understanding. My best friend is always telling me to believe in the impossible and trust the Universe and all that kind of stuff. I've spent my whole life looking for the facts. What is it that makes the lightest cake batter or the richest flavor? That kind of thing. There's always science to explain it, right? If you look for an explanation, there usually is one."

"Of course," I say, because it's the only thing I can get out past the alarm bells roaring in my head. If Dean heard this conversation, he wouldn't give me a chance. He'd wipe her memories and send her away without so much as warm feelings left.

She bites her lower lip before continuing. "But, ever since I've arrived in Magnolia Cove, it's left me questioning that." My heart stops beating. It skips two entire beats before picking up again in a frantic staccato. "Maybe there's more than meets the eye, after all. Maybe even some secrets that seem hard have an explanation too."

My mind races. I want to tell her everything. I want to let magic flow through my fingertips and swirl the surrounding air with the scent of honey, make the shrubs glisten and the stars shine. But I can't. The risks are too great, not just for me, but for the entire community.

"A vacation can make you feel that way."

Loose hair whips across her frown and drags my jacket

back from her shoulders. The clothing makes her feel a part of Magnolia Cove in a way her designer outfits haven't. I can see her here, hair always windswept by the ocean breeze, an apron tied around her waist. I want it desperately, but it's not reality. She's going to return to the city soon and I'll be nothing more than a fleeting memory. At best, I'll be a charming anecdote in her next article. After tonight, not even that seems likely.

"It's not just the vacation." Her lips press into a thin line before continuing. "I travel frequently and have seen some unique locales, but Magnolia Cove is different. You're different. I've wondered the entire time what the answer is, but maybe—" Her eyes drift to the cliffside again, where the ocean roars. "Maybe it has been magic all along."

Dean's glare flashes through my mind. Jas' anxious voice telling me everyone is worried that Alex will discover our secret. The way friends rallied behind me while others stared in concern at the council meeting.

This is the moment I've dreaded. The moment I've known was coming. I've been like a bug fixed on a light, trapped by the blare of an oncoming train. I can't hurt everyone around me who relies on this island's secrecy. Dean was right. If Alex saw my reality, she'd reject me anyway. With the moon out and my emotions running high, I can feel control slipping. I take a deep breath, trying to center myself.

"Alex," I say, gentle but firm. "What you've seen is what Magnolia Cove wants you to see. We're an island that runs on tourism. Everything here is a gimmick."

"A gimmick?" she repeats in a hollow voice.

I shove my hands into my pockets. Goosebumps rise on my arms, but it's not the cold that's cutting through me. It's what I know I need to do.

"Yes, a gimmick." The words feel like molasses in my mouth, thick and bitter, but I push on. "The quaint town, the magical pastries, the feeling that everyone knows you. It's all carefully crafted to give visitors a sense of wonder, to make them feel like they've stepped into another world."

Alex takes a step back. Her lip wobbles, and that nearly breaks my resolve, but I hold firm. "No, I don't believe you. I came here expecting to find a gimmick, but I've found something real. I know it."

Everything in me wants to reach out, to pull her close and tell her the truth. But I can't. I force myself to meet her gaze, to keep my voice steady as I deliver the final blow.

"I'm sorry, Alex. But this... us... it's not real. You're leaving soon, and I'm just... I'm part of the Magnolia Cove experience."

Tears well in her eyes, and I see the moment her heart breaks. It mirrors the shattering in my chest.

"You're just pushing me away," she says through gritted teeth. "I know about the trouble you've been in before. I've seen the news articles."

My breath catches. The council had wiped all of those articles. A few stray papers must have slipped through the cracks. She doesn't know the story's truth. It hits me that she's still choosing to be here with me, regardless. Alone in the dark.

Despite my past, she trusts me.

I want to scream, but there's no turning back. If I don't get her to leave, get her to hate me, then the council will wipe her memories. I guess I'm selfish because I don't want her to lose everything we've shared. Even if she only sees it as jaded. And I definitely don't want her to end up harmed.

"Then you know Dean is my... parole officer." It's the closest role I can think of.

"Parole officer?" she mumbles.

"Magnolia Cove made me a deal. I become the face of the island, sell their gimmick of magical baked goods, and flirt with pretty tourists—" I let that sit for a moment, long enough that the hurt wells in her eyes again. "Then Dean will cut my time sooner."

"No," she whispers, so quietly the wind swallows it.

"Yes, Alex. This is a game I'm playing. I want to return to Paris one day, hopefully sooner than later. Whatever it takes to gain my freedom, I'll do it."

"No. You're not... This isn't..." She crosses her arms as another brutal gust of wind whips over us. "I could write an article destroying the Whisk."

It takes everything in me to dredge up the bitter, careless laugh I throw at her. "You think I care about the Whisk? I don't."

I do, of course. It's my life's work. My greatest passion.

And the greater implication—that I don't care about her —hurts even more. She releases a sob and shakes her head like she can't believe it. Then she scrunches her sleeve-covered hands against her eyes like she wants to wipe the night away.

The sight of her pain is almost unbearable. Every instinct screams at me to take it all back, to pull her close and tell her the truth. But I can't. I have to see this through, for her sake and for the safety of everyone in Magnolia Cove.

"I'm sorry, Alex," I say, fighting to keep my voice steady. "But you've been searching for the truth and you've found it. It's just uglier than what you wish to believe."

She looks up at me, her eyes red-rimmed. "I don't believe you. The Ethan I know wouldn't—"

"The Ethan you know doesn't exist." Each word feels like a dagger in my heart. "He's a character I play, nothing more."

Alex takes another step back. It's grown nearly cold up on the cliff, and the distance between us emphasizes it. "So every moment," she says, "every conversation, every... every touch. That was all fake?"

I force myself to nod even as the magic within me roars. I

can't stand the lies I'm telling her, the hurt I'm dishing out. "I'm good at what I do."

She stares at me for a long moment, searching. Then she shakes her head. "You're hiding something. This island is hiding something. Pushing me away isn't the answer."

"There's nothing to hide, Alex. It's just Magnolia Cove, doing what it does best—creating an illusion."

She stares at me for what feels like an eternity, her face slowly transforming. It's like watching an earthquake gradually crack a street, slowly swallowing the surrounding buildings. Then she scrubs at her face and straightens. She peels my jacket off and thrusts it at me. The polished, careful food writer reappears. The woman who'd walked off a ferry in pumps and a pressed shirt.

She turns and storms down the path, fists clenched at her sides.

I watch her go, each step feeling like a physical blow. The magic in the air seems to dim, and the beauty of the night turns to ash.

I've done what I had to do. I've protected Alex and the town, kept our secrets safe. But the weight of what I've lost settles over me like a shroud. I can't help but wonder if the price was too high.

"Very convincing, Hart." I startle as Dean steps out from the shadows.

My muscles tense, and magic surges through me. "How long have you been listening?"

"Long enough." He shoves his hands into his pockets and stares out at the dark sea. "I had to make sure you handled things. This is a delicate situation." A beat of silence passes, and I'm too angry and broken to respond. "I'm not personally against you, Ethan."

There's more humanity in his voice than I've ever heard, but, for once, I don't care. I've been searching for something that mattered for years—I chased it around the world with baking. I've spent over a decade perfecting each recipe, trying to capture a taste of home, something that matters. Now I've found it—her—the real thing. And I let her go. No, worse, I shattered her. I let her walk away with tears slipping down her cheeks.

The jacket has cooled from her warmth, and I can feel myself changing, feel the magic taking over.

"Hopefully, I've finally given enough," I mutter, more to myself than to Dean.

As I turn to leave, the weight of the night settles over me. I've protected our world, our secrets. I've even protected Alex from having her mind touched by magic. But at what cost? Every thudding footstep down the path leaves me wondering if I've made the biggest mistake of my life.

Alex

~∽∽~

The sun hasn't risen yet, but I've given up on sleep. My eyes sting, raw from a night of silent tears. I furiously shove the last of my clothes into my suitcase. My dry cleaner will never forgive me for the damage I'm causing them, but I can't help it.

My phone buzzes for what feels like the hundredth time—Tish again. I can't bring myself to answer. Of course, now the cell service decides to work. Magnolia Cove kept me off the grid when I wanted connection, and now that I want silence, it delivers full bars. One word of pity from Tish, one mumbled 'Oh, honey,' and I know I'll crumble. Sending her a text at all was impulsive. Like every decision I've made since arriving in Magnolia Cove.

God, I'm such a fool.

How did I let this happen?

Part of a summer in a picture-perfect town, and suddenly I'm nursing a broken heart like some lovesick teenager? I've spent years building walls, protecting myself from this kind of pain. From this kind of emotional compromise. And for what? To let my life come crashing down over a small-town baker with secrets in his eyes and magic in his hands?

Magic. The word sticks in my throat, bitter and mocking.

My article on the Whisk is overdue, and I don't know how I'm going to write it. Part of me—the part that's all jagged edges and hurt—wants to tear Ethan's bakery apart. Because despite everything he said, I know he loves that place. You can't fake the way his eyes light up when he talks about a new recipe, the gentleness in his hands as he kneads dough, his patience with Jas.

Then there's another part. The part that wants to write something so bland, so utterly forgettable, that Vivian will relegate it to the back pages of the magazine. She'll be furious. There goes my promotion. There goes everything I've worked for, all because of some man who would rather lie to me than trust me.

Because everything Ethan said to me on the cliff was a lie.

A knock at the door startles me from my spiral. I glimpse myself in the mirror—puffy eyes, tangled hair, yesterday's clothes rumpled from a sleepless night—and I consider not answering. Another knock sounds, and with a sigh, I rise and open the door a crack.

Zoe stands on the other side, her dyed hair braided into a pompadour. She shoves her hands into a maroon leather jacket. "Hey, City Girl, mind if I come in?"

I step aside wordlessly, letting her enter.

She slings her backpack onto the overstuffed chair in the corner, then walks around the room, closes all the blinds, and pulls the curtains tight. I cross my arms as she peeks through the last set of blinds before closing that window and leaving the entire room in the dim glow of a single lamplight.

"I have something to show you." She walks over to her bag. "Can't get caught, though. Would hate to end up on restriction. Mia wants to see the Grand Canyon next year, you know what I mean?"

I drop into the boudoir chair. "I have absolutely no idea what you mean, and you must know that."

She grins at me, then meets my eyes, her expression dropping into a frown. From the backpack, she pulls a bakery box from the Whisk. She grabs a chair, swings it around backward, straddles it, and then opens the box between us.

The air fills with the scents of the bakery, of Ethan. Spicy, rich cinnamon and boldly sweet vanilla. Zoe pulls a red velvet cookie out and offers it to me. "Taste this."

I don't know what she's trying to tell me, but I've had no ice cream to nurse my broken heart with, and a cookie will do just fine. The bite I take isn't a food-editor-saving-her-palette-sized bite, but a third of the cookie. It's soft and cakey, the sweetness perfectly balanced with a subtle depth and hints of rich cocoa. Ribbons of luscious cream cheese burst across my tongue with the first bite. I take a shaky breath after swallowing and swipe a tear away. "It's delicious. It tastes like one of Ethan's recipes."

Zoe gives a sharp nod, then looks over her shoulder, as if locking the room down wasn't enough. When she turns back, she raises her hand over the cookie. A shimmer appears beneath her fingers, pale gold and undulating.

My hands tremble, and I fumble to keep from dropping the cookie. "What did you just do?"

"You know what I did." She's as serious as a delayed flight in a country closing its borders. "Taste it now."

I lift the cookie and smell it. It looks the same—a perfect treat from Ethan Hart's kitchen. I bring it to my lips and pause for a second before taking another more modest bite.

The flavor remains—it's still luscious and pillowy with perfect crisp edges and a dynamic, balanced flavor. But it's also changed. My shoulders relax, my breath comes easier. It tastes like kicking heels off after a long day. Like snuggling down into your favorite blanket and putting on a comfort show.

I gasp and look up at Zoe again. "How?"

She grips the chair's back so tightly her knuckles turn white and rocks it slightly off its feet. "Seriously? That's the question? Here Ethan and I have been running around like caffeine-addicted squirrels in a coffee bean factory trying to hide this from you, and now that it's handed to you on a silver platter, you don't know the answer?"

The remainder of the cookie shakes in my grip. I release two heaving breaths before I find the word. "Magic."

I look at Zoe, squinting as though I can see the magic. She's the same colorful, purple-haired woman I met earlier in the summer, though. No glittery light or moonbeams or whatever should be there.

"So that's the big secret Magnolia Cove is hiding?"

Zoe nods, her usual mischievous smile replaced by something more solemn. "We've protected our world for a long time. Not telling non-magical humans is kind of our number-one rule."

"Then why are you choosing to tell me?"

Her eyes meet mine, steady and sure. "Because I trust you. And I can't have you leaving here with a head full of lies."

The words hit me like a punch to the gut. Trust. The very thing Ethan couldn't give me.

"And Ethan can do magic too?" I ask, barely above a whisper.

Zoe grins, a spark of her usual self returning. The lights in the room brighten, and the sweet, vanilla smell of golden cookies fills the air. It's like now that I've seen a bit of magic, she thinks I'm ready to watch dishes come to life and start singing and dancing as they prepare me dinner. I'm not. I'm barely able to breathe, and I haven't lowered the hand holding the cookie. It's just frozen there, and I'm gripping the treat so hard crumbs dust the floor.

"Ethan can do a lot more than me. He's a rare one, even for those of us around here. Was born with more magic. Most of us can just polish things up a bit, enhance flavors, that kind of thing."

It all makes sense now. The too-perfect town, the way the food here always tastes a little better, a little more comforting. I know, with a certainty that surprises me, that I would never betray their secret. Zoe was right to trust me.

But someone crucial didn't.

Zoe must read my expression because she straightens. "Whatever the hell he told you, it was meant to scare you off. It wasn't true, Alex."

A sad smile tugs at my lips. "That makes sense. The problem isn't even the magic, really. I get having people you need to protect. The problem is that you trusted me, but Ethan didn't."

Zoe's shoulders slump, and the speed of her speech increases. "Ethan has more magic than most of us, and more riding on his actions. It's not my place to say what, but he's forbidden to share."

"And you're not forbidden to share?" I ask.

Zoe's face falls. It doesn't suit her—the down-turned lips and flared nose. Finally, she sighs. "I am as well."

I want to hug her but also cry. "Thanks, Zoe. It means a lot, and I swear it, your secret is safe with me. But... you understand why I have to leave, don't you?"

Her eyes glimmer, and I'm not sure what I'll do if she cries. She nods. "I couldn't convince you to stay if I baked you a lifetime supply of those Hopeful Tarts, could I?"

I laugh, but it comes out more like a sob. "No, I'm afraid not." I wonder how much the magic has tugged on my emotions. If the Hopeful Tart's magic made me put my cynicism aside and see the future in a new light. But that's not real life. I'm not the person who gets a happily ever after. I'm the one who orchestrated them for others. "My sister needs me, and I'm not"—I hold the cookie up—"magical. This isn't my world, Zoe."

I stand. I have so much to think about and process. But if this proves anything to me, it's that Ethan and I never were meant to be together. I'd already thought we had insurmountable differences. Him having magic? That just turned them into the Pacific Ocean between us. We had a sweet moment together, one that gave me hope, even without magic involved. But vacation is over. It's time to catch a plane and return home.

Zoe eases off the chair. "He cares about you, Alex."

"And I care about him. A lot." So much that I know I'll never write a piece destroying the bakery he's built from the heart. Even if it costs me the raise I desperately need. Maybe I'll see if I can get a few of Jas's Courage Cupcakes before I go because I'm going to need them. "But we can't make this work. Ethan knows it too, or he'd be here."

Zoe's face crumples, but she pulls me into a fierce hug. She smells like old books and caramel, and I somehow know magic isn't enhancing any of it. It's just Zoe. "You're always welcome back in Magnolia Cove, City Girl. Always."

As I pull away, I can feel the tears threatening again. "I'm going to miss you."

"I'll miss you too. Though not as much as someone else will miss you."

"He should have told me that."

She sighs but pulls me into another hug. "Yeah, he should have."

* * *

189

Hours later, after the ferry, a taxi, and making it through the perils of TSA, I'm on a plane, twinkling lights of cities passing below me. Silent tears track down my cheeks, but I don't wipe them away.

For once in my life, I'd found magic. Real, honest-to-god magic. But it wasn't mine to keep. It never was. I was foolish to believe I could reach for more, that I deserved more than the life I'd carved out for myself.

I have to go home. Salvage my job. Pay for Missy's tuition. Focus on her happiness. That's what I'm good at—taking care of others, making sure others live their dreams.

Even if it means sacrificing my own.

As the plane carries me farther from Magnolia Cove, I close my eyes. In my hand, I'm clutching a Whimsical Whisk cookie bag. The gold logo has a whirling whisk surrounded by glitter. If I squeeze it tight enough, I swear I can feel magic humming against my skin. A reminder that, for a brief, shining moment, I touched something extraordinary.

And maybe, just maybe, a tiny part of that magic will stay with me.

Alex

I'm glad I had time to stop by Celestial Sips before my meeting with Vivian. The familiar scent of herbs and spices wraps around me, a stark contrast to the heavy humidity already building in the morning air outside. The shop is mostly empty, save for Tish and me, the silence only broken by the soft clink of china and the whisper of pages turning.

Golden light dances across the worn wooden tables, cast by star-shaped lanterns hanging from the ceiling. Their intricate patterns throw constellations onto the walls, transforming the cozy tea shop into a magical realm.

"I'm an idiot to be so heartbroken over a guy I just met," I mutter into my cup of tea.

Tish reaches across the table, her hand warm on mine. "Love doesn't have a timeline, sweetie."

I scoff. "Who said anything about love?"

Tish gives me a look that says she's not buying it for a second. "Let me give you a reading. It's been a while."

It's been more than a while. I'd only allowed her to read the tea leaves for me that first time when I'd interviewed her about the shop for *Gastronomy Eats*. I'd never believed in magic. Before.

Now, the word 'magic' sends a pang through my chest, reminding me of the way morning sunlight spilled into the Whisk and the heavenly smells that permeated the air.

"Fine." I swallow all but the last of the tea, then push the cup toward her. "Work your witchy wonders."

Tish's eyes sparkle as she swirls the lingering tea and leaves around the cup, then gently turns them over onto the saucer. We wait in silence for a minute while she allows it to settle.

I remember doing this the first time. How she put so much attention and focus on it while I maintained a strictly neutral, professional expression. I'd known then that magic didn't exist. Things have changed, and despite my lingering skepticism, I'm watching the cup just as intently as Tish.

She flips it over and tilts it toward the light. "All right, let's look. Immediate future first. I see... hmm... a message with financial gain coming your way."

"You sound like a fortune cookie," I snort, but there's no real bite to it. After Magnolia Cove, I'm not sure what to believe anymore.

Tish shoots me a mock glare, then returns her attention to the cup. "Hush, you. There's more. I see... a journey. Not a physical one, but a journey of the heart or the soul. And... oh, interesting."

"What?" I lean forward despite myself. Even if everything she's said so far sounds as vague as a newspaper horoscope, with a little imagination, anyone could make those details fit their lives.

"There's a bear. I don't see that one very often."

She's frowning at the cup, and I shift in my seat, trying to remind myself I don't believe in this stuff before I say, "And what does that mean?"

Knowing my luck, it means my life is about to become unbear-able. Okay, that's a corny thought, even for me, but my muscles tense, waiting for whatever premonition this rare sign means.

"Strength and endurance." Tish tilts the cup again, into the light. "The ability to endure challenges. What's strange is that the bear isn't alone. There's another figure beside it. That could mean that you're about to experience support from another. Or that you've already gone through trials."

I sit back in my seat. "That's awfully vague, Tish."

She sets the cup down, her gaze locking with mine, and there's something in her eyes that makes my skin prickle—a knowing look, like she sees right through me. "The leaves don't give specifics, darling. They just point the way. It's up to you to walk the path."

Her words hang in the air, oddly resonant, like a truth I didn't realize I needed to hear. My phone buzzes, snapping me out of my stupor. I glance at the screen, groaning as I read the message. "Speaking of paths, I've got to go. Vivian's waiting, and I'm pretty sure 'magic and tea leaves' won't work as a valid excuse for being late."

Tish stands, pulling me into one of her massive hugs, her arms warm and comforting. "Go get 'em, tiger." I linger there for a heartbeat, the warmth of her embrace a stark contrast to the rush of reality waiting for me outside. Reluctantly, I pull away, gather my things, and head for the door.

"And Alex?" Tish calls, her voice softer now. "Keep your heart open. You never know what might find its way in."

I offer a small smile, a fleeting moment of reassurance before stepping out into the buzz of a New York City morning. The sidewalk stretches before me like an endless runway, and I slip back into my "city" clothes—crisp blazer, pencil skirt, my hair pulled tight into a severe bun. The contrast stings. I miss the comfortable t-shirts and flour-dusted aprons from The Whimsical Whisk. I miss the wind in my hair and

Ethan's gaze softening when he looked at me... No. I shake the thought away. *Focus, Alex.*

When I finally make it up to the office, Vivian's waiting, arms crossed, her perfectly pressed blazer creasing just slightly in the middle. "Well, well. Ms. Sinclair in the flesh. Please, take a seat."

I shut her office door behind me, standing tall despite the knot in my stomach, then walk across the room with measured steps. I perch on the edge of a chair, spine ramrod straight. "Vivian, I—"

"Save it," she cuts me off, her voice icy, clipped. "You've been back for days, and still not a single word about The Whimsical Whisk. Care to explain?"

I swallow hard, the words stuck in my throat. "It's... complicated."

"Complicated?" Her perfectly manicured nails click against her watch face, the sound sharp, demanding. She once embodied everything I wanted to be—independent, polished, well-paid. Alone. That loneliness hits me hard, like a punch to the gut. It might work for her, but I can't live like this. Not anymore.

"You once wrote a stunning piece about haute cuisine during a cholera outbreak, Alexandra. What could possibly be 'complicated' about a small-town bakery?"

If only she knew. If only she understood the magic that hums beneath the surface of this place, how the people care for each other like a family, how a baker with gentle hands and a guarded heart sacrifices everything to protect a world she barely comprehends.

I take a breath, choosing my words carefully. "This assignment was different from any other, and I'm still processing the experience. I went there expecting a gimmick and found something real."

Vivian eyes me with suspicion, her gaze sharp as a blade, but she doesn't interrupt.

"I want to do the experience justice."

"You've pushed every deadline I've given you on this piece. Missed meeting after meeting. More than doubled your travel time. If you were a less-valued writer or had neglected any of your other articles, I'd fire you."

I gulp at the implication, my heart thundering. Magic or not, bills still have to be paid. I can't afford to be fired.

"I've remained patient because you're one of our best," she continues. "But you've exhausted the patience I possess."

"I know, and thank you. I promise I'll have the article to you by the end of the week."

"By midnight tomorrow." She pinches the bridge of her nose. "And it had better be the best damn thing you've ever written. This piece needs to sing, Alex. It needs to sell enough copies of *Gastronomy* that our board stops breathing down my neck about budget cuts and 'adapting to a modern media landscape.' I need you to take some of The Whimsical Whisk's magic and put it into an article, understand?"

I flinch at the word *magic* but nod. "It will. I promise."

She holds my gaze for a long moment. "Good. Now, is there anything you need from me to get this done?"

"No, I—" I begin, but she's already reaching for something on her desk.

"In that case, this came for you earlier." Vivian holds out an envelope.

I take it, confused. There's no return address, only my name, *Gastronomy Eats, c/o Alexandra Sinclair*. Thick red letters are stamped across the front: *First Class. Overnight.*

"Thank you, Vivian. I won't let you down."

She skims her eyes over me, then lifts her chin. I can't tell if it's an expression of faith or simply a *you know the way out.*

Either way, I take the cue and leave as gracefully as I can manage.

When I'm in the elevator, finally alone, I open the envelope.

A whiff of something familiar fills the air. Cinnamon and the rich tones of overpriced vanilla... Ethan. My hand shakes as I fish the papers free.

I find myself staring at an application form for a scholarship program.

My eyes widen as I scan the details. It's for the exchange program in Paris that Missy has been dreaming about. A full-ride opportunity that would cover everything—tuition, travel, food. It's perfect. And the deadline... it's tomorrow.

Tears spring to my eyes. *He did this.* Ethan found this opportunity and made sure it reached me in time.

A realization hits me like a tidal wave. I never believed the lies he told me on the ridge overlooking the ocean. I knew Zoe was right—they were falsehoods meant to push me away. But some doubt must have lingered in the back of my mind. A fear that real love didn't exist. That it was always a lie. A false magic that comes crashing down.

Ethan loves me too. But we can't be together because of our differences. Because of the secrets he keeps.

I clutch the envelope to my chest just as the elevator dings open on the ground floor. Stepping out of the lobby and into the smog and rain of a New York City day, my chest aches with joy for Missy, with relief over the financial situation, but even more deeply with a pain that threatens to swallow me whole.

In that moment, standing in the middle of a busy sidewalk, I have never felt more alone.

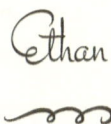

Ethan

The bakery used to be my sanctuary. Now, it feels like a prison. It's been weeks since Alex left, but the ache in my chest hasn't dulled.

I knead the dough with more force than necessary, trying to lose myself in the familiar motions. Trying not to think about the feel of Alex's skin beneath my palm, the rich tenor of her laughter, the heartbreak in her eyes that last night.

The quiet that once brought me peace now feels oppressive, every silence a reminder of what I've lost.

The blue of early morning has brightened just enough to softly illuminate the empty booth by the window. Alex's booth. A fresh wave of pain sweeps through me. I turn away, forcing my attention back to the task at hand.

The back door bangs open, and I don't need to look up to know it's Zoe. She bursts in like a hurricane of color and noise, her bright clothing a stark contrast to my mood.

"Morning, Boss!" she chirps. "Hope you're ready for some tunes, because I've got a playlist that'll knock your socks off!"

Before I can protest, she's already fiddling with the speaker, and an upbeat tune rings through the space, a chorus of voices echoing the lead singer. I grit my teeth, resisting the urge to tell her to turn it off. I know what she's doing—trying to pull me out of my funk. Part of me appreciates it, but a larger part wants to wallow in my misery.

"Zoe," I start, but she cuts me off with a wave of her hand.

"Nope, you said you don't want to talk about it. Fine, then we'll sing instead."

I shake my head and return to my work. The dough has started to take shape, but it feels hollow and overworked—like everything else in my life right now. I hate the looks of pity the Cove's residents keep giving me. It was better when I first moved here, when they were all wary of me. At least then I could pretend I didn't care what they thought.

I reach for another bowl, but my hands slip, and it crashes to the ground. The shattering sound echoes through the bakery, drowning out even Zoe's music.

I stare at the mess, frozen. Something inside me has cracked along with the bowl. The speaker goes silent. The next moment, Zoe is by my side, her brow furrowed.

"Ethan," she whispers, all traces of her joking tone gone. "Enough already. Call Alex and tell her the truth. Tell her how you feel."

I clench my fists and blink away unshed tears. "How I feel doesn't matter."

"Of course it matters!" Zoe yells. Despite her anger being directed at me, I appreciate the ferocity of her friendship—how quickly she jumps to my defense, even when I don't deserve it.

"She can't know who we really are," I say, the words bitter on my tongue. Our relationship was impossible from the beginning. I was selfish enough to think it could be a summer fling, too blind to see how badly I'd hurt Alex in the end.

Zoe's next words hit me like a physical blow. "She already does."

I jerk my head up to meet her gaze, my heart hammering. "You told her?"

Zoe has the grace to look sheepish. "I couldn't let her walk away thinking you're just an asshole who manipulated her and broke her heart, Ethan."

I inhale sharply, the scent of yeast thick in the air. I think of the Council, of Dean's stern warnings. The consequences of revealing our magic to outsiders blare through my mind—memory wipes, exile, or worse. And Zoe could face those consequences because of my choices. My heart clenches.

My control is slipping, magic crackling at my fingertips. "Do you know the trouble you could get into?"

"Some things are worth the risk," Zoe shoots back, squaring her shoulders. "Alex is trustworthy. She could belong here—I think she wanted that, even. I showed her magic, and she barely flinched."

I run a trembling hand through my hair. "You told a journalist our greatest secret."

"I told Alex," Zoe snaps, her eyes flashing. "Not a journalist. Not a human or a city girl. Alex. And she accepted it—accepted us."

Her words hang in the air, heavy with implication. I turn away and brace myself against the counter. There's so much left to finish before the Whisk opens, and now none of it seems important. Alex knows. She knows, and she didn't run screaming. She didn't immediately publish our secrets to the world or call the police.

"What have you done, Zoe?" I whisper, but there's no real anger in my voice. Just exhaustion.

Zoe bends down and gathers the broken shards of the bowl, tossing them in the trash before answering. "I did what you were too scared to do. I gave her a chance to understand. To choose."

I close my eyes, remembering the way Alex's lip trembled

on the cliff. "She might accept magic in general, but she'd never accept me."

Before I can blink, something cold and sticky splatters across my cheek and neck. I sputter and wipe the frosting away, staring in horror as it drips from my apron. Zoe stands before me, empty bowl in hand, her jaw jutted out.

"What the hell was that for?" I gasp.

Zoe slams the bowl down hard enough that it vibrates the counter. "Because words aren't working, pity isn't working, and being Little Miss Sunshine isn't working either. You need a wake-up call. You're head over heels for Alex, and you're just sitting here like a week-old muffin instead of doing something about it."

I yank a towel free from its hook and scrub at my face. "Everything with Alex was foolish for so many reasons. I've been heartbroken before, and I'll get over it."

Zoe steps closer. "You forget, I met you right after everything went down with Sarah. You were messed up then, sure, but not like this. Back then, you were heartbroken over your destroyed career and shattered dreams. This time? You scarcely think about the consequences. You would've given up everything—the Whisk included—to protect Alex." She pauses, her gaze softening. "Don't think Mia didn't tell me about you asking her to help find a scholarship form for Alex's sister."

I freeze, and frosting drips from my arm, plopping onto the ground. "What of it?" I say, hoping it comes out nonchalant.

"What of it!?" Zoe throws her hands up, and I'm afraid she's about to chuck something else at me. "Infatuation is when you're attracted to someone. Maybe you had that with Sarah—fine. But love? Love is when you care about someone else's well-being and happiness over your own. You love Alex, you big dummy, and you're just going to stand here and give that up because you're scared."

I stare at her—at the fuchsia headscarf tied over her purple hair, her fierce brown eyes, and the gleaming tattoos with Mia's name written in script across her bicep. I want to deny her words, to argue with her. But Zoe knows me too well.

"It doesn't matter," I whisper. "Even if you're right—even if I do love her—I'm different. More dangerous than most magical beings. You know that. I can't risk—"

"Doesn't Alex have a right to make that decision?" Zoe slams her fists against her hips. "That one's got a good head on her shoulders. I think you misjudged her, and honestly, Ethan, you owe her better than what you gave her."

Her using my actual name makes me come up short, pausing before I respond. I want to argue—but deep down, I know she's right.

As I stand there, covered in frosting and reeling from Zoe's words, I think about Alex—her sharp intellect, the way she could dissect a recipe with a single taste, her keen observations of the town and its people.

How protective she was of her sister. How determined.

I've done her a disservice by making this decision for her—by forcing her out before she even had a chance to understand. The realization sits heavy in my chest, along with a flicker of something I'm almost afraid to name. Hope.

What if I explain everything—my past, the magic, the dangers—and she accepts me? What if I've found someone who actually wants me? Loves me?

I've been a coward. Letting her go was easier than facing the truth. Maybe the person who needed a Courage Cupcake all along was me.

"You're right, Zoe," I say. "She deserves the truth. All of it."

Zoe's face breaks into a crooked, triumphant grin. "Now that's what I like to hear! What's the plan, Boss?"

I take a deep breath and square my shoulders, knowing the

only answer. "I'm going to have to get permission from the Council."

Zoe nods. "You've got this, Ethan. Just share your heart. You've been a member of this community for years—you deserve more credit than you get. And for what it's worth, I think Alex is going to surprise you."

Her belief is almost enough to bolster my own. My heart is thudding again, though first, I have to clean up. Damn, I was an idiot. Zoe literally had to throw a bucket of sugared butter at me to snap me out of it.

"Thanks, Zoe. For everything."

She waves a hand dismissively, but her cheeks flush. "Yeah, yeah. Besides, you always think you're so terrifying, Ethan. You're nothing more than a teddy bear—I'm just bringing you down a notch."

I snort a laugh. "That's deserved."

"I agree. Now, I've got the Whisk under control for the morning. You get cleaned up and gather the Council. You've got a foodie to win back!"

As I head to the bathroom to change, a spark ignites in my chest. I've made mistakes, but maybe the situation isn't hopeless. Maybe I'm not.

* * *

The Council chamber feels colder than usual as I stand before the group, my heart pounding but my resolve firm. I've just finished explaining my request, and the silence that follows is deafening.

Councilwoman Frome scoffs, breaking the tension. "And why, Mr. Hart, even if we agreed to give Ms. Sinclair an opportunity to join our community, should we trust you with such a monumental task? Leaving the island before your term is up? Revealing magic to a human?"

I meet her gaze steadily. "Because I'll take Dean with me."

A ripple of surprise runs through the room. Dean's shock reaches me without me even looking at him.

"I know the risks. I know what I am and what I've done before. But I think I've proven myself in my time here. And I'm willing to vouch whatever goodwill I've gained on Alex. We can trust her. I'll accept any conditions, any restrictions you deem necessary, if it means I have this chance."

The Council members exchange glances, a silent conversation passing between them. Finally, Councilman Hawthorne leans forward. "And if she rejects your proposal?"

I swallow hard, pushing down the knot in my throat. "I vow to maintain myself, even if that happens. Plus, Dean will be there if magical intervention is necessary."

Another long moment of silence follows. Then, slowly, Councilwoman Evelyn nods. "Very well, Mr. Hart. You have our permission, with Dean as your... chaperone."

I fight a shiver at the word. I've wanted nothing more than to break Dean's shackles since I arrived at Magnolia Cove. Now, I'm walking into a cage—but with a bigger purpose. Because Alex is worth the sacrifice.

As I leave the chamber, Dean falls into step beside me.

"You know," he says, his voice gruff but not unkind, "I've always wanted to see New York City."

"Sounds like you're in luck."

Dean's face falls into its normal scowl, but I can't help the hope rushing through me. If even Dean Markham is willing to give me a chance, maybe this isn't as impossible as I thought.

Maybe there's a real shot at making things right with Alex.

Alex

The rain pounds against the windows, matching the tumultuous beating of my heart. Missy is on her way out, umbrella in hand, a whirlwind of energy and independence. She's grown so much. For so long, I've seen her as my little sister—needing help tying her shoes, needing someone to watch out for her. But that's not who she is anymore; she's a woman carving her own path.

"Don't forget your mail," she calls over her shoulder, tossing a stack of envelopes onto the coffee table. "I'm staying at Jenna's tonight. I'll bring more milk home tomorrow."

As the door clicks shut behind her, I sink onto the couch, fingering through the pile until I spot it—the latest issue of *Gastronomy Eats*. My breath catches as I take in the cover. The photo is of Ethan, but not like the Foodie Frenzy image where they'd photoshopped him into wrinkle-less perfection, completely fake.

No, in this image, the light is golden and hazy, his face slightly out of focus, but the wrinkles around his eyes are visible. He had just finished laughing at a comment I made. The actual subject of the photo is his hands—strong and sure, rolling out a pie crust.

There's magic in this picture, just not the kind Magnolia Cove hides.

With trembling fingers, I flip to my article and read. The words flow like a river, a story not just about the Whisk and Magnolia Cove, but about the true magic of food and the stories it crafts. The tale of a little boy creating courage with a mixer, a woman who brings her exuberance and passion into her relationship with customers, a fourth-generation pie recipe passed down with love. And at the heart of it all: Ethan—a man who makes room for every person around him to shine. Who absorbs bits and pieces of everyone he meets, his empathy and compassion transforming them into food that embodies what baking should be about. Home. Comfort. Love.

It's the best piece I've ever written. Even Vivian agreed with that. Despite taking a different angle, she was pleased with it. I never once mentioned magic or Magnolia Cove's secrets. Because the real magic, I've realized, is the people. The relationships that create the food. Everything else is just... extra.

I close the magazine, my shoulders rolling back even as my heart thunders anxiously. Alongside the article, I'd turned in my resignation. Missy got her scholarship—I smile at the thought—but I still have bills to pay. I'm terrified, but it's time to pursue my own passions. *Tell Me Something Sweet* is getting a revival, focusing on heart-filled recipes. I'll pick up some freelance work too. When Missy moves, I'll get a roommate. I don't have it all figured out yet, but for once, that feels okay.

A knock at the door jolts me from my thoughts. I laugh softly, setting the magazine aside. "Forget your keys again, Missy?"

But when I swing the door open, it's not my sister standing there.

It's Ethan. And Dean.

My heart stops, then surges back to life at double speed. They're both dripping wet, rain plastering Ethan's curls to his forehead. His eyes are a storm—hope, fear, longing—each emotion battling for dominance. I drink in the sight of him, too stunned to believe he's actually standing there.

I remember how I silently cried into my pillow for weeks after I came back. I scolded myself for it, for the foolishness of it all. Writing the article had brought the best parts of Ethan back to me—his soft smiles, the thoughtfulness in his pale blue eyes. But now, standing in front of me, he's real again, and I realize something else. The man I created for that article wasn't him. He was a myth.

This is the real Ethan.

The man who laughed about his Parisian neighbor's dislike of him—as long as she kept sharing her recipes. The man who drives his grandfather's classic car and fits in as well at a farmer's market as he does on the cover of a pop-culture magazine. The man who has secrets and shame he hid from me. The man who pushed me away.

"I... Can we come in?" Ethan's voice is soft, uncertain.

I step back and gesture for them to enter. "Of course."

There's a pause as Dean closes the door behind them. Ethan sweeps his gaze across the apartment. If I'd known he was coming, I would have shoved more stuff into closets. It's not messy, exactly, just lived in and blaring with the details of mine and Missy's lives. A few cameras sit on a desk in the corner, magazines are stacked haphazardly on a side table, and baking paraphernalia litters the counter.

Ethan's attention returns to me, and I forget about the apartment. About Missy or my career or Magnolia Cove or anything else.

I'd longed to see him again. Even for just a moment.

"There's something I need to tell you—show you, really," he says so quietly I strain to hear the words over the rain's clatter. "Sorry for bringing Dean along. I had to."

"Because he's your parole officer?" The words slip out before I can stop them. Ethan smells like vanilla, even five hundred miles from Magnolia Cove. He looks like home, and it makes my heart ache.

Ethan grimaces. "Not exactly. You know about magic already, but—"

"She what?" Dean speaks for the first time since walking in. His eyes have turned into ebony beads, but then he sighs and gives Ethan a nod before jerking his black leather jacket off and turning toward the windows like he has to shift his focus to the city's illumination in the distance to stop himself from intervening.

A shiver runs down my spine. I hadn't fully considered the weight of knowing Magnolia Cove's secret—and what it could mean for me.

Ethan exhales a long, slow breath. I ache to curl into him, to touch his skin just to make sure he's real. His eyes lock onto mine with a fierce intensity, as if trying to forget Dean's presence in the room. "What I said that night on the cliff... I was trying to push you away, to keep you and the others safe."

"I understand that now," I say softly, my voice tight with the sting of old wounds. "But it still hurts that you didn't trust me." I'd known it since Zoe's magical display at the B&B, and I'd suspected it long before. Ethan's jaw clenches, his eyes flicking away like he can't bear to face the truth. That lack of trust had been our undoing.

"Yeah, but there's more." Ethan turns away from me, his profile carved in tension. The man who's captured my heart— the ClipClop heartthrob, the baker with a soul warmer than his banana bread—is standing in my shabby apartment. He clears his throat, and when he looks at me again, his eyes are raw. "I was a coward. I was afraid if you knew who I really am—"

"I want to know." My voice is barely a whisper. I want to reach out, to brush the curls from his forehead, to let my fingers trace the curve of his cheek, the line of his lips. A part of me is terrified that if I don't touch him now, he'll vanish into thin air. "I've always wanted to know you, Ethan. Maybe at first as a journalist, but later..." I glance at Dean's stiff shoulders, his stance like a sentinel by the window. If only he weren't here for this conversation. "Later, I wanted to know you—the real you."

"The real me scares some people. It has... before."

"This isn't before," I whisper, as if I could erase Dean from the room. I know better, of course—our apartment is smaller than a breadbox. "You can trust me."

"I think I can. And I want to show you. But—no matter what happens, promise me you won't panic. That's why Dean is here. He won't let anything bad happen to you, okay?"

I glance quickly at Dean, who's moved closer, his focus entirely on Ethan. Ethan steps away from me, his gaze dropping, head bowed like he's bracing for something heavy.

I want to tell him that whatever it is, I can handle it—that I've already seen the real him. But before the words leave my mouth, something happens.

It starts with a shimmer in the air, like heat rising off sun-baked pavement. Ethan's skin pulses with a soft golden light. The air around us crackles, charged with energy, thick with the sensation of a storm on the horizon.

The same glistening magic Zoe had shown me in Magnolia Cove surrounds Ethan, but this is different. It's not just a spark—it's alive, vibrating with power, as if every cell in his body is singing in a language I can't understand but feel deep in my bones.

His eyes, normally pale blue, flare with an inner fire, the color swirling in a whirl of gold and amber against a sea of endless black. The transformation is breathtaking, and yet, utterly terrifying. I can't look away.

I hold my breath, watching as his fingernails stretch into sharp claws. Golden-brown fur ripples across his skin, replacing his flesh in an instant. His hands, once soft and gentle, elongate into massive paws, tearing through his clothes as they fall to the floor in shredded remnants.

My heart pounds, the world shrinking to this moment— this impossible, breathtaking moment.

Where Ethan stood a moment before, there is now a massive bear. For a terrifying second, I choke on my breath. Dean dashes forward, positioning himself between the bear and me.

I stumble back toward the kitchen, my back colliding with a stool. It topples with a thud. The bear cowers, ducking its head, its brows furrowing together.

That's when I realize—it's not a bear I'm looking at. Not really.

"Ethan?" I whisper.

The bear's eyes look nothing like Ethan's. But somehow, I know it's him. And he's not frightening. This is Ethan—the gentlest man I've ever met. The baker who coaches a boy who needs to see that you don't have to fit the mold to matter. The man who hands out free treats to neighborhood kids and talks about baking with passion and vigor.

And a person who can change into a bear, apparently.

I realize it changes nothing. I spent a night wrapped in his arms without a drop of fear. Gulping down a deep breath, I straighten.

This is still Ethan. And even though a wild creature takes up the limited floor space in my apartment, I know it—he— won't harm me.

I step forward, slowly raising my hand. Ethan-the-bear pulls back slightly. Dean moves even closer, and I want to shove him away. Ethan wouldn't hurt me. He only ever fought to protect me, and now that all the secrets are out, there's nothing left between us but the truth.

My hand lands on the fur around his face, and the bear shudders, but I twine my fingers into the thick strands. "I see you, Ethan," I say, my voice steadier than I expected. "And I'm not afraid."

In a blink, he's back—human, naked, and crouching on my cheap laminate floor. I barely notice the lack of clothing as I drop to my knees beside him and pull him into a fierce hug. His arms wrap around me, strong and sure.

"Okay," Dean's gruff voice breaks the spell. "This is outside of my pay grade. Where's your bathroom?"

I point vaguely down the hall, not taking my eyes off Ethan. As soon as we hear the bathroom door close, I cup Ethan's face in my hands and tilt it up, trying to make out the bear in his features, but I can't see it anymore.

"This is what you were hiding?"

Color flushes his cheeks. "I'm dangerous, Alex. Even other people with magic fear shifters."

I study his strong jaw, the length of his nose, still searching for the powerful creature I just witnessed. All I see is Ethan— kind, gentle Ethan with his soft blue eyes and a worried frown. "You don't seem dangerous to me."

"You're not... afraid? Or disgusted?"

I shake my head, a smile tugging at my lips. "Ethan, I've heard you wax poetic about sugar grades. I've listened to you patiently teach Jas how to pipe the perfect rosette. The most dangerous thing about you is how easily you've made me fall in love with you. If this is the only thing standing between us, then there's nothing standing between us at all."

His eyes widen, something blooming within them, making them sparkle. "Alex, I—"

My mouth finds his, cutting off his words. The kiss is gentle and warm. "I love you," I say when I finally pull back. "All of you. The baker, the shifter, the man who unfairly won the *Baking Bonanza* with his kitschy shortcake." He chuckles, and my fingers find their way into his curls. "I love the man who can transform into a bear just as much as I love the man who can transform simple ingredients into something magical. You're not dangerous to me. You're... You're the first time I've felt like I've found home."

Ethan's breath catches, and then he pulls me into a fierce embrace that I can't help but think of as a bear hug.

"I love you too," he whispers against my hair. "Can you forgive me for being such a fool?"

"You don't even need to ask."

As the rain continues to pour outside, I hold on to Ethan, marveling at the magic I've found—not in food that tastes like comfort or an island fit for a calendar, but in finding another soul who has allowed me to see past the surface and loving him, not in spite of it, but because of it.

Ethan

The early morning sunlight filters through the gauzy curtains of Alex's small New York apartment, casting a warm glow over the cramped kitchen. I perch on a barstool, watching Alex move about with practiced ease. The scent of coffee mingles with something savory—eggs, I think—and for a moment, I'm transported back to mornings at the Whisk.

But this isn't Magnolia Cove. This is Alex's world, and somehow, impossibly, I'm still a part of it.

I can't stop marveling at her—the way her hair catches the light, the curve of her smile as she hums to herself, how she moves with such surety in this tiny space. She saw me last night. All of me. The fur, the claws, the truth of what I am. And she didn't run. She didn't scream. She accepted me.

I try not to fixate on Sarah's rejection years ago. On how her reaction set off my magic and put me out of control as the bear. How I created a path of destruction through the human town, getting myself sentenced to a decade in Magnolia Cove under the watch of a warlock whose magic could snuff mine out if necessary. But even thinking about that now reminds me of Alex's soft eyes as I told her the story, of the way she tangled her fingers with mine as if to say she'd stand by me, flaws and all.

My gaze drifts to the stack of cookbooks teetering atop her fridge. We've already discussed a few of the titles I recognize— debated the finer points of which chef has the best glaze. I've accepted that we still don't agree on everything recipe-wise. The easy flow of our conversation, the depth of her culinary knowledge—it all leaves me in awe. I've found the person I've spent my entire life looking for.

And then there was the way she touched me after Dean left last night, her fingers tracing my jaw, my shoulders, as if committing every inch to memory. The first passionate time we made love—burning off weeks of desire and separation— then the slow build of the second time. Her soft moans, the way she whispered my name in the darkness. That she knew all of me, saw all of me, and still wanted me at her side. I remained awake even as she drifted to sleep in my arms. I had scarcely dared to hope for all this.

I'm pulled from my reverie as Alex slides a plate in front of me. It's a frittata, dotted with cherry tomatoes and herbs. Nothing fussy or pretentious—just good, honest food. It's so perfectly us I can't help but smile.

"What?" Alex asks, a hint of playfulness in her voice.

I shake my head, still smiling. "Nothing. Just... happy."

She leans across the counter, her face close to mine. "Me too."

I capture her mouth in a kiss. She humors me, running her fingers through my hair, then pushes me back and points at the plate. As we eat, I can't help but wonder about the future. Dean's gone to a hotel—he's given me the weekend after ensuring the situation was "safe." But after that? The Council hasn't said they'll let me off early, and the Whisk... Well, it still holds my heart. I've realized I don't want to leave it—or Zoe, or my customers, or Jas.

But Alex and I have overcome bigger obstacles, haven't we? We can handle a long-distance relationship. As long as I have her in my life, I'll make it work.

"I haven't thanked you yet," Alex says suddenly, pulling me from my thoughts. "For finding the scholarship for Missy."

I wave it off even as heat creeps up the back of my neck. "It was nothing, really."

"No," she insists, her eyes serious. "It really meant a lot." She pauses, taking a deep breath. "I have some news too. Maybe not as big as 'I can transform into a bear' news, but pretty big."

My heart skips a beat, but I steady myself. Whatever she says, I'll accept it. She could hold space for the big, hairy truth of me—I can definitely do the same for her. "Oh?"

Alex meets my gaze, her eyes swimming with something. "I quit my job."

I nearly choke on my coffee. "What? But... I thought you loved food writing?"

"Food writing, yes," she says, a wry smile playing on her lips. "Food journalism, with all its negatives? Not as much anymore." She shrugs, trying for nonchalance but not quite hitting it. "Besides, I've been wondering if my traveling days might be behind me."

Hope blooms in my chest, but I try to temper it. "Where are you thinking of settling down?"

Alex hops up and gathers the empty plates. She takes them to the sink before answering. "Well, there is this island you might have heard of. But maybe not—it's not very well known." Her eyes sparkle as she continues, "Looks like it was photoshopped. Beautiful stretch of beach, and a bakery I've heard makes damn good cinnamon rolls. It even impressed a snooty food journalist who used to write for *Gastronomy Eats*."

My breath catches in my throat. "You'd move to Magnolia Cove?" I want to add 'to be with me,' but the words stick.

Alex turns on the faucet, her voice pitched slightly higher than normal. "I mean, I don't know if there's an application or something. Maybe I wouldn't even get in and—"

I stand, joining her around the counter. My heart is pounding, but for once, it's not with fear or doubt. It's with wild, unbridled hope. "If you want to move to Magnolia Cove, I can get your application approved." The words come out with more certainty than I feel, but I know I'll fight like hell to make it happen. Besides, the Council will probably prefer to keep Alex close now that she knows our secret.

As soon as the words leave my mouth, new dreams form in my mind. I see Alex working on *Tell Me Something Sweet*— her food blog that I'd obsessively read after she left, the writing so authentic and rich and so decidedly Alex that it had only made my heart ache more. I picture her taking photos, experimenting with recipes, while I run the Whisk. Our evenings and nights spent together, sharing meals, sharing stories, sharing a life. The vision is so beautiful it's almost painful to contemplate.

Alex's voice pulls me back to the present. "Missy leaves in a few weeks," she says, a hint of nervousness still in her tone. "After that, if it works for you, Mr. Hart..." She pauses, a smile tugging at her lips. "Then yes, I think I'd like to try out living somewhere slower-paced and, as you once said to me, reigniting some passions."

Joy surges through me. I jump to my feet, move around the counter, and whirl Alex around in a giant hug, lifting her off her feet.

Her laughter, bright and beautiful, fills the small kitchen. "Is that a yes?" she asks, her arms wrapped tightly around my neck.

I set her down gently, cupping her face in my hands.

"That's a yes, please," I murmur before capturing her lips in a kiss that holds all the promise of our future together.

When we finally part, both a little breathless, Alex grins up at me. "All right then, Chief," she says, her eyes sparkling. "Looks like you've got yourself a new neighbor."

I can't help but laugh, pulling her close once more. "Welcome home, Alex," I whisper against her hair. "Welcome home."

Alex

EPILOGUE: SWEET PROMISES

The bell over The Whimsical Whisk's door jingles as I push it open, the familiar scent of vanilla and cinnamon permeating the air. It's been a year since I first stepped foot in this bakery, and now it feels more like home than my apartment in New York ever did.

"Alex!" Mia calls out, jumping up from our usual booth. Rachel, Rihanna from the library, Tom, who works at the Bait and Tackle shop, and Violet, Hazel's granddaughter, all have their hands wrapped tightly around steaming mugs of coffee. Everyone is eager for the update.

"Sorry, I interrupted book club," I say, sliding into the booth.

"Well, what's the news?" Rachel leans forward, her eyes sparkling.

I can't help the grin that spreads across my face. "That was my agent. It's official. *Tell Me Something Sweet* is going to be more than just a blog. We have a book deal!"

The table erupts in cheers and congratulations. Tom raises

his mug in a toast. "I guess we know what our next book club read will be!"

I laugh, shaking my head. "It's not really fiction, though."

Mia catches my eye, a mischievous glint in her gaze. "Well, it's not the full truth either." We all share a knowing chuckle at that.

"Besides," Rihanna adds, "once your café next door is up and running, we won't have to worry about getting kicked out early when the place closes."

As if on cue, Ethan appears from the back with Jas in tow, both wearing flour-dusted aprons that make my heart skip a beat. Even after all this time, the sight of Ethan still takes my breath away.

"You're all welcome to stay as late as you like," Ethan says, his blue eyes crinkling at the corners as he smiles. "But us bakers have to rise at the crack of dawn. What's all this celebrating about?"

I meet his gaze, and his eyebrows raise. With just a look, he knows. "Seriously?"

"Seriously!" I say.

"Oh my god, Alex, that's amazing news." He rushes over as I stand, then twirls me around the room. Jas squeals and claps his hands as my friends cheer in the background.

Before Ethan puts me back on my feet, Zoe bursts through the kitchen door. "All right, bookworms, as much as I enjoy watching Alex make googly eyes at our resident Teddy Bear baker, some of us have a date with a pillow and a Netflix queue." She saunters over to Mia and throws an arm around her wife's shoulders. "Besides, if I have to watch Ethan and Alex dance around the dining room for one more minute, I might go into sugar shock. And let me tell you, that's saying something coming from a pastry chef."

Ethan rolls his eyes good-naturedly. "Zoe, behave."

"Never," she grins, then winks at me. "Someone's gotta keep things interesting around here, right, City Girl?"

"Right."

Everyone seems to buzz with the desire to share my news. I know Zoe will dance and shout the loudest of anyone, but I can also tell she's tired. Mia gives me a wink as she leads her to the door. She'll break the news, and I can expect fluorescent, rainbow cupcakes later in the week to celebrate.

As the group disperses, Tom asks, "When are you going to marry this one, Ethan?"

Heat rises to my cheeks as Ethan and I exchange a look. Fear and desire blend in his eyes—a complexity I've come to understand and love. He's still cautious sometimes, but always honest with me. I laugh, trying to deflect. "Who says I'm ready to settle down?"

The group chuckles, and Ethan's shoulders relax.

Jas bounces out last of all, but not before making me promise to teach him another food photography class over the weekend.

"He's really grown to love you," Ethan says as he locks the door.

I'm looking at the Whisk—at the chalkboard sign with tomorrow's specials written in Ethan's careful script, the pristine awning that looks like it belongs in a holiday movie, the twinkle lights I convinced Ethan to add, the framed *Gastronomy Eats* article that hangs just inside the door. The bakery has become a symbol of everything I've found in Magnolia Cove.

"You know," I whisper, "I think I've grown to love it too. All of it."

Ethan's hand finds mine, his fingers intertwining with my own. "Interested in a walk on the beach?"

We make our way to the familiar cliff where he once broke

both our hearts. Now, it's a symbol of how far we've come, of the trust we've built.

We're quiet on the walk up. I'm thinking through all the details of a real-life book deal, a cookbook with my name on it, my stories pressed between the pages, recipes filled with love and comfort that others might make and share.

Ethan keeps smiling at me softly, occasionally pressing a kiss to my temple.

"Did you tell Missy yet?" Ethan asks as we look out over the water.

I lean against him until I can hear the steady rhythm of his heart. "Not yet. I spoke to her this morning; she finally got service again. I swear, her tour with the orchestra still terrifies me, but I'm so proud of her."

"She's so much like her sister," Ethan says softly, his arm tightening around me.

I flush, my heart swelling with love for this man who's become my home. "Hey, Ethan?" I say, my voice barely above a whisper.

"Yeah?"

I take a deep breath, gathering my courage. "If you ever asked me... to marry you, I mean. I'd say yes."

His gasp catches in the wind, then he pulls me closer. He presses a kiss to my hair and sighs into my skin. "I guess I'll have to think of something spectacular. Can't have a world-famous blogger and newly minted author not have a story worth telling, can I? Popping the question on our trip to Paris this autumn would be too cliché. So that's out."

I chuckle and curl down against his warmth.

We stand there in comfortable silence, watching the sunset paint the sky in hues of pink and gold.

As the world darkens and ocean waves roll in a lullaby, I realize dreams do come true. That happily-ever-afters do exist. Even for people like me.

Standing here in Ethan's arms, our future stretching before us like an open road, I feel a sense of peace I've never known before.

I think again about the book I'm getting published—a love letter to small-town life, magical bakeries, and food made with heart and soul. It's not the exposé I came here to write, but it's infinitely more precious. It's the story of how I found my home, my heart, and myself in this enchanted corner of the world.

As the first stars begin to shimmer in the deepening sky, I close my eyes and make a silent wish. Not for fame, not for success, or any of the things I once believed would fill the void. No, this wish is simpler. I wish for more nights like this one. More mornings waking up to Ethan's undivided attention, his warmth filling the space between us. More lazy afternoons spent strolling the beach, the salty air brushing against my skin. More recipes born from nothing but a scrap of paper and a tin box of forgotten notes. More moments—wild, messy, and unfiltered—that make life feel real.

Because, for the first time, I've discovered the secret ingredient to a truly magical life. It's not about unraveling mysteries or chasing the next big headline. It's about opening your heart. To love. To community. To the quiet, everyday magic that we so often overlook but is always there, waiting to be noticed.

Wrapped in Ethan's arms, I smile. I've found my happily-ever-after, and it's sweeter than any I could have imagined.

* * *

Loved *Whisked Away*? There's more magic waiting for you!

Don't leave Magnolia Cove just yet—I have something extra special for you! If you want to see what happens when

Ethan and Alex take on Paris (*romance, pastries, and one last heart-melting twist!*), plus get a **recipe book filled with 24 recipes inspired by the story**, grab your exclusive bonus content here:

https://dl.bookfunnel.com/bxnnj7ld3l

I can't wait for you to read it!

I'm so grateful you spent time in this world with me, and I hope you carry a bit of its warmth (and maybe a few new favorite recipes) with you.

Until next time—sending you love, magic, and just the right amount of cinnamon sugar.

-Noel

Next Book

Loved *Whisked Away*? Don't leave Magnolia Cove just yet!

If you couldn't get enough of small-town charm, swoony banter, and a sprinkle of magic, you'll adore *Love by the Book*. Dive into Rhianna and Eli's story—where a free-spirited librarian and a buttoned-up rare book curator clash over matchmaking gone wrong, an enchanted library, and feelings they never expected.

Opposites attract? Check.

Friends-to-more (with plenty of mutual pining)? Double check.

A guaranteed happily-ever-after? Always.

Grab a cup of tea, curl up with a good book, and return to Magnolia Cove for a love story that's as charming and spellbinding as the town itself.

Pick up *Love by the Book* today and fall in love all over again!

Jas' Courage Cupcakes

When Jas first made these all on his own, carefully frosting each one and selling them under a hand-painted sign reading *Jas' Sweetcakes*, Ethan couldn't have been prouder.

But the first time Ethan took a bite?

The citrus hit first—bright, bold, impossible to ignore.

Then the honey cream cheese frosting—smooth, grounding, just the right amount of sweet.

It was Jas in dessert form—vivid, warm, and completely unforgettable.

INGREDIENTS:

For the Citrus Cupcakes:

- 1 ¾ cups (220g) all-purpose flour
- 1 ½ teaspoons baking powder
- ½ teaspoon baking soda
- ½ teaspoon salt
- ¾ cup (170g) unsalted butter, softened

- 1 cup (200g) granulated sugar
- 2 large eggs
- 1 tablespoon orange zest
- ¼ cup (60ml) fresh orange juice
- ½ cup (120ml) buttermilk
- 1 teaspoon vanilla extract

For the Honey Cream Cheese Frosting:

- 8 oz (226g) cream cheese, softened
- ½ cup (1 stick, 113g) unsalted butter, softened
- ¼ cup (60ml) honey
- 2 cups (240g) powdered sugar
- ½ teaspoon vanilla extract
- Pinch of salt

INSTRUCTIONS:

The Cupcakes:

1. Preheat oven to 350°F (175°C) and line a muffin tin with cupcake liners.
2. In a medium bowl, whisk together flour, baking powder, baking soda, and salt.
3. In a large bowl, beat butter and sugar until light and fluffy.
4. Add eggs one at a time, beating well after each addition. Stir in orange zest and vanilla.
5. Mix in half the dry ingredients, then orange juice and buttermilk, then the remaining dry ingredients. Mix until just combined.
6. Divide the batter into liners, filling ¾ full, and bake for 18–22 minutes, until a toothpick inserted comes out clean.

7. Let cool completely before frosting.

The Frosting:

1. Beat cream cheese and butter together until smooth and fluffy.
2. Add honey, vanilla, and a pinch of salt.
3. Gradually mix in powdered sugar, beating until creamy and spreadable.
4. Swirl generous dollops of frosting onto each cupcake.
5. Garnish with a drizzle of honey or a little extra zest for flair.
6. Take a bite. Feel a little bolder.

A LITTLE EXTRA COURAGE:

- For extra citrusy punch: Add ½ teaspoon orange extract to the batter.
- For a bakery-style finish: Pipe the frosting into tall, dramatic swirls.
- For a daring twist: Sprinkle with crushed candied ginger—because bravery takes spice.

These Cupcakes Might Not Be Magic...
But they *do* taste like courage.
And maybe, just maybe, that's enough.

* * *

Loved this recipe?
There's more where that came from! Grab the **free bonus content** with 23 more recipes from the book—including

Tish's Zodiac Cookies, the **Hopeful Raspberry Tart**, and yes... **Ethan's top-secret Cinnamon Rolls** (shh, don't tell him I shared).

You can download the whole set for free right here: https://dl.bookfunnel.com/bxnnj7ld3l

Acknowledgments

Writing a book is never a solo endeavor, and *Whisked Away* wouldn't exist without the incredible people who have supported, guided, and encouraged me through every twist and turn of this journey.

First, to Milly—my brilliant editor, my coach, my cheerleader. You've been with me through so many books, but this one, this *genre leap*, felt like stepping into uncharted waters. And yet, you were there, steady as ever, reminding me that I *could* write romance, that I *did* know what I was doing (even when I doubted it), and that these characters—flawed, wonderful, and deeply lovable—deserved their story. You love them every bit as much as I do, and that means the world.

To Jacki, my sister and my rock. Without you, this entire series wouldn't exist. Thank you for believing in me, for talking through wild ideas, and for reminding me (often) that I should keep going even when the path felt uncertain.

To my husband, who stands beside me through every creative obsession, every late-night writing sprint, and every moment of self-doubt. Your unwavering support means everything.

To my daughter K, baker extraordinaire and someone who inspires me every single day. You may not have made a Jackson Pollock countertop like Ethan, but you've certainly done it to my Hedley & Bennett apron! Ha! Thank you for all your insight on baking, for helping me brainstorm, and for testing recipes for the cookbook. I love you!

To Hamala, my phenomenal line editor, for smoothing

out my words with such care, and to Bring Design for crafting the most gorgeous, perfectly suited cover for Whisked Away. I could stare at it forever.

To Megan, my eagle-eyed proofreader, who screams at me in messages (in the best way) when my words make her feel things—and who catches every little thing I miss.

To Mallory and Jill, my incredible coaches, for helping guide this series from the very beginning. Your insight and encouragement shaped so much of what *Whisked Away* became.

To my friends, who have cheered from the sidelines, read my books, and believed in me from the very beginning—you have no idea how much that means.

And finally, to you, my lovely readers. Writers don't exist without readers, and I am endlessly grateful for each and every one of you. Thank you for believing in magic, in love, and in the joy of a good book. I hope *Whisked Away* brings you as much delight as it brought me while writing it.

With love and gratitude,

-Noel Bailey